D0477169

SPECIAL MESSAGE TO READERS

THE ULVERSCROFT FOUNDATION
(registered UK charity number 264873)

was established in 1972 to provide funds for research, diagnosis and treatment of eye diseases. Examples of major projects funded by the Ulverscroft Foundation are:-

- The Children's Eye Unit at Moorfields Eye Hospital, London
- The Ulverscroft Children's Eye Unit at Great Ormond Street Hospital for Sick Children
- Funding research into eye diseases and treatment at the Department of Ophthalmology, University of Leicester
- The Ulverscroft Vision Research Group, Institute of Child Health
- Twin operating theatres at the Western Ophthalmic Hospital, London
- The Chair of Ophthalmology at the Royal Australian College of Ophthalmologists

You can help further the work of the Foundation by making a donation or leaving a legacy. Every contribution is gratefully received. If you would like to help support the Foundation or require further information, please contact:

THE ULVERSCROFT FOUNDATION
The Green, Bradgate Road, Anstey
Leicester LE7 7FU, England
Tel: (0116) 236 4325

website: www.foundation.ulverscroft.com

THE RELUCTANT GUN HAND

Jake Worthy's sole shooting offence was firing back at a crooked gambler in a Tucson saloon. For that, he received a six-month prison sentence. Bushwhacked along the trail home, he is taken in by a gang of thieves led by a beautiful, money-crazed woman named Yvonne and cold-eyed killer Billy Davenport — and it is join up with the gang or be left in the mountains to die. As Jake is led along a trail of treachery, violence and murder, his hopes of finding a peaceful life seem increasingly remote . . .

LOGAN WINTERS

THE RELUCTANT GUN HAND

Complete and Unabridged

LINFORD
Leicester

First published in Great Britain in 2013 by
Robert Hale Limited
London

First Linford Edition
published 2014
by arrangement with
Robert Hale Limited
London

A catalogue record for this book is available
from the British Library.

ISBN 978–1–4448–2143–7

Published by
F. A. Thorpe (Publishing)
Anstey, Leicestershire

Set by Words & Graphics Ltd.
Anstey, Leicestershire
Printed and bound in Great Britain by
T. J. International Ltd., Padstow, Cornwall

This book is printed on acid-free paper

1

Jake Worthy wasn't so angry with them for shooting him, but they didn't have to shoot his horse as well! Montero was the horse's name — a big, deep-chested red roan with legs that might have been a little slender for its bulk, but carried him well. Now it lay dead on the rocky ground beside him. Jake had scooted up next to the animal on his wounded leg, meaning to use the animal's body as a rampart, but no more shots rang out, no shadowy figures approached him in the haze of twilight.

His first thought was that it must have been Indians, for he was deep into Apache territory, but no Indian would deliberately kill a fine, very usable horse.

The other matter was the weapon that had been fired at him. He knew by the snap of the bullets, their rapid loosing that it was no primitive musket-rifle, but a quite new repeater, possibly one of the spanking new '73 Winchesters which were starting to appear on the far boundaries of the country, though not yet in profusion. The new, much improved lever-action rifles were still too expensive for most men to purchase because of their rarity.

Jake himself carried a now outdated Spencer .56 repeater for which it was getting harder to find ammunition. The weapon had served him well, however. In fact it had saved his life more than once, and he had grown accustomed to it. He had become more aware lately of how quickly time was passing him by, but a man seems to pause at a certain point in his life, and if he finds himself comfortable enough, he no longer pursues change just for the sake of it.

It was growing rapidly dark; the sunset was a wash of orange and crimson against the sky above the White Mountains. Jake had planned on making Rio Lobo this evening. Now he could no longer be sure that he would make it through the night.

His eyes continued to search the rough country around him, a land devoid of vegetation except for stands of nopal cactus and Spanish Dagger plants. The shadows were gathering in the folds in the hills, and though the earth beneath him was warm, the sky was darkening. He had to get up and move. The furrow carved by a passing bullet in his thigh was painful, but it had nearly stopped bleeding. He knotted his bandanna around the wound and tried to stand, his eyes still searching the perimeter. He had neither heard nor seen anything, man or animal, for the last hour as he lay behind his slowly stiffening horse.

That did not mean that no one was out there.

He could even now be in the sights of some patient rifleman, but he did not think so. It was a gamble to move, a gamble to remain where he lay. One thing was certain, he was not going to reach Rio Lobo on this night as he had planned. Becky Holland would just have to wait, but then she was used to waiting for Jake Worthy. He frequently arrived late, sometimes not at all. He had intended to put a stop to all of that this time.

He had gotten off lightly with only a six-month prison term, but the six months had seemed like six years. Jake was tired of the game, tired of peering through bars, spending lonely nights trying to remember what he had profited from years of scrambling around. Nothing, nothing at all with the possible exception of Becky Holland. He meant to make it up to her now if he could ever get off this damned desert!

He reflected that on his release from prison he should have just bought a stagecoach ticket instead of trying to ride through the White Mountains, but he was accustomed to having a horse between his legs when he traveled, and there was a sense of freedom to it so opposite to the depressing, dehumanizing days wasted away in a thick-walled cell. A stagecoach's confines seemed a continuation of the prison, although he knew the thought was ridiculous.

He returned to what he had always been — a free man alone without shackles or restrictions — out of habit and because of the sheer joy riding free lent him.

He paused for a while to look down at the body of Montero, then began trying to salvage what gear he could. There was no way he was going to tote his saddle across this rugged land with a bum leg, and he left it regretfully. He snatched up his bedroll. He would have a rough time of it out here without blankets. Then he slid his well-worn Spencer repeater from the scabbard, tugged his canteen from beneath Montero's shoulder and started on with night coming, unsure of his destination on this savage, settling evening.

Jake knew that the moon would be rising sometime after ten o'clock — a waning quarter moon which provided only meager light to travel by, but hopefully enough to prevent him from plunging into some unexpected gorge. The moonlight would be some help. Jake did not know this country except in generalities.

Ahead lay the foothills, uninhabited as far as he knew, and then the twenty-mile wide desert salt flats. Beyond these, in the east, the land grew green and fertile again. Not too terrible a ride with water and a good horse. Except now he was afoot, and the distance seemed a menacing stretch of inhospitable land. If there was water along the way, he did not know where, and he doubted it. There would be no shade, of that he was certain, and little in the way of wildlife. Beyond that, in the green strip, lay Rio Lobo where Becky Holland waited. Would she be crying, wringing her hands, or simply shrugging, knowing that Jake had disappointed her once more. Tiring of it completely, would she turn her attentions to another, more settled man?

Why couldn't he have simply stepped on to a stagecoach?

A hard head and a lust for freedom — well, he had his freedom now, he thought, as he staggered and lurched along on a wounded leg, alone in the desert night in unknown territory. The land was rough, rocky slopes with scattered cholla cactus. There was no visible trail down the hillside or none he could make out at this hour before sundown.

As to the reason Jake had gotten himself thrown in prison, it was something that might have been considered trivial only a few years back. But civilization, as they called it, had crept into the western lands, and in Tucson they had civic committees as they called the collection of fat men in town suits and their fat wives, who mostly sat around in the town hall sipping tea and disparaging the rough and tumble men who were the true founders of the town and others like it across the West.

They were civilized people and wished for everyone else to be as they were.

Tucson now had not only a town marshal and a corps of deputies, but also a judge and a courthouse. There had to be some way to rein in what they considered the excesses of the rough old-time crowd who had blazed their trails for them, fought the Indians and pushed the frontier this far west. Now they were viewed by the late-comers as a rowdy bunch of tobacco-chewing, hard drinking, gun-toting menaces to society as they saw it.

One day these stiff-shirted people would rule the West. Jake hoped he would be in his grave before then.

Sitting in on a poker game at the Fairview Saloon, he had caught the dealer palming cards and called him on it. The gambler, whose name was Ned Quirk, had pulled a nickel-plated derringer from his vest and raised it in Jake's direction. Jake kicked his own chair backward, drawing and firing as he fell. It wasn't the best position to be aiming from, but he had gotten the gambler. It was not a killing shot. The bullet from Jake's pistol had literally parted Quirk's hair, grooving his scalp from front to back. The damage was trivial, but the blood flowed copiously and Quirk's face was a crimson mask as he fled the table.

They had to arrest Jake Worthy, of course. They wanted to try him for attempted murder, but witnesses told the truth of the matter and, in the end, the judge — who had also lost some table money to Quirk — sentenced Jake to a relatively light six-month sentence for negligent discharge of a firearm within the city limits. Of course, in the old days, Jake wouldn't have even been arrested, it being a clear case of self-defense. But those days were gone, Jake supposed. He and others of his ilk just did not fit in with the new ways coming.

The stiff shirts in Tucson were

already calling for banning handguns, gambling, prostitution and sales of liquor in the city. Who knew if they'd ever get their way, but they were having a grand time doing what they did — it seemed to make them feel superior to the rag-tag sort.

When Jake had done his time, he wanted nothing more than to ride the wide land which was exactly as it had always been. The stiff-shirts hadn't yet found a way to tame it.

Becky Holland who had waited patiently in Rio Lobo, had written him twice a week while he was in prison, and her letters had helped him pass the time there. She did say once, 'But, Jake, it seems I've been waiting half of my life for you to come home and settle down. Please hurry.'

He had been trying — until this.

He could no longer see the sad body of Montero as the shadows of night settled and he trudged farther away from the ambush site. Once he thought he saw a distant light, but it was quickly extinguished, like the brief flaring of a damp torch. Jake tripped over an unseen rock and went to his knees and elbows against the stony ground. It was foolish to go on. He might step off into some unseen ravine or sinkhole. It was already tough going on his wounded leg. Suppose he were to break a bone?

Reluctantly, then, he rolled out his bed, intending to catch some sleep before the moon rose later and the light was better for traveling. It took him fifteen minutes to kick the small rocks away from the piece of ground he had chosen, and still, of course, he did not get them all. It was an uncomfortable place to sleep under a sky that promised to grow cold as the stars blossomed across its vast, dark face.

With his wounded leg still alternately throbbing and burning and the stony ground nudging his back, he slept uncomfortably, but did manage to catch a few hours of sleep. His eyes flickered open as the moon rose from the desert distances. The way it

shimmered across the silver-gray landscape was almost magical. It brought
little light, but after the near total
darkness of a few hours before, its
strange glimmering illuminated the
rises and declivities of the long hills
enough to convince Jake Worthy that it
was safe enough to travel on; besides,
his sleep had not been exactly restful
and he knew that the night would grow
no more comfortable.

Rising, he nearly collapsed again
immediately. His wounded leg had
stiffened up on him. There was nothing
for it but to work through the
awkwardness and the pain, hoping
movement would loosen it up again.

He started on, limping, staggering,
stumbling toward the desert floor
beyond. He wondered now how far he
would be able to walk even after he hit
flat ground. Tomorrow would arrive
with searing desert heat and he was a
wounded animal. The next time he
would take the stagecoach like a tamed
man. It had been bred into him that a

man takes care of himself rather than trusting himself in other hands, no matter what. He was beginning to find flaws in that theory of self-reliance.

A narrow arroyo forced him to go upslope to detour around it, not wanting to have to slip down to its bottom and then be forced to scramble up again. His leg was not capable of such a climb.

He was alone on a desert mountain range in a haunted night, wading through intermittent pools of moon shadow cast by boulders along the way.

And then, suddenly, he was not alone.

Who they were, where they could have come from, Jake Worthy could not guess, but there they were directly ahead of him, standing spaced out along a rocky ridge. There were three of them wearing long coats. Their hats were tugged down far enough that their eyes did not show in the moonlight, only dark suggestions of them.

Not a single one of the shadowed

apparitions moved as Jake dragged himself farther up the slope, needing to circle the head of the arroyo. He approached the motionless watchers as they waited. What else was there to do? He could not run; he had to get to higher ground. If they wished to kill him, they would have already done so — three riflemen vaguely silhouetted against the darkness against one injured man back-lit by the moon like a shooting gallery cut-out. He had no chance but to approach them, hoping they were not as menacing as their appearance suggested. Three black figures appearing out of the desert night, unmoving, unspeaking — Jake limped and stumbled on, nearing them, wondering where they had come from, what sort of men they could be, abroad in this desert wasteland, and above all what they wanted with him!

Because they obviously had business with him, or thought they did, since they waited, frozen in a menacing tableau along the dark ridge, neither calling out nor gesturing. Nor did they come to assist him as he struggled and scraped his way up the rocky hillside half-dragging his wounded right leg.

Jake Worthy considered — he had no known enemies in this vast wasteland, but neither did he have friends in the dry wilderness area. Whoever these watchers were they must have already formed their course of action, whatever that might be. With luck, Jake thought, in a gunfight he might be able to get one of them, possibly two, but warring with three riflemen in the darkness on unsteady ground was a dangerous proposition. There was no way Jake could hope to escape without at the very least finding himself badly perforated, if that was the intent of the bunch. He stumbled on, trusting to chance, for that was all there was to trust to.

He was within a dozen strides of them when a strangely familiar, reedy voice finally called out, 'We'd appreciate it if you'd drop your rifle for now,

Worthy! And you can also unbuckle your gunbelt. No sense in taking any chances.'

No. There wasn't.

Instead of dropping it, Jake lowered his rifle to the rocky ground. He did not believe in mistreating his weapons, women or horses. Unbuckling his Colt, he placed it beside his Spencer repeater. One of the men came forward, his Winchester lifted in the area of Jake's stomach and leaned over to pick up the guns. Nearer now, Jake could see that the man did indeed have eyes. One of them had a strange cast to it, and both bulged like a frog's. He was stocky, his body seeming to be a little sloppy beneath the dirty clothes he wore.

'All right, Jake, let's get tracking,' the man with the voice that seemed almost familiar said, and the four of them began to climb the hillrise in silent unison, the frog-eyed man walking behind Jake Worthy, his rifle still leveled.

Topping out the rise, Jake looked

down at the moon-illuminated valley beyond. A stone house, with wings stretching out on either side rested on a table of flat ground near the base of the rising cliff beyond. Someone had wanted his comfort out here on this naked land. Here and there you would stumble upon a sagging, weather-grayed shanty or a small stone cabin, but a house of this size was a true rarity in the White Mountain area. The windows, Jake noticed, were only rifle slits designed to hold off Indian attackers. The front yard was barren and dry, only a scraggly, undernourished oak tree growing there.

The four men dipped down into the shallow ravine and clambered up the other side to approach the house. One of them called out to let anyone inside know that they were arriving. If the person, whoever it was, manning the house had a nervous trigger finger, the sight of four shadows approaching the house from out of the night could set him off.

Instead, walking through utter silence, with only the sound of the men's boot leather whispering against the rough ground to be heard, they approached the front door as the moon rose higher, the night wind began to funnel down the mountain passes. Jake still had said nothing. He had no idea what these men's intentions were, but they seemed to have no interest in conversation just then. They were keeping him alive; there was no point in bringing him back to their den to kill him. There would be time for talking later, then.

One of Jake Worthy's abductors — or rescuers, depending on how you looked at it — rapped loudly on the heavy plank door and was answered from within by a muffled voice. The door swung wide and the four tramped in.

Jake, who had seen a few things in his life, was totally stunned by the appearance of the woman who had opened the door for them. She had raven dark hair falling across her shoulders and breast, and bright blue eyes. Nearly six feet tall, she wore a black dress displaying some sort of red sash from shoulder to hem and embroidered white lilies on the bodice. The toes of highly polished black, pointed shoes showed beneath the hem of her dress.

One of the men swept off his hat and kissed her — a gesture which the woman seemed to tolerate rather than relish. By the lantern light in the living room, sparsely furnished and low-ceilinged, dominated by a vast native stone fireplace which no one living in this country could ever have found enough wood to use, Jake saw that the man, a complete stranger to him, was tall, rather thin, wore a neatly trimmed dark mustache and had hawkish eyes which seemed to challenge the world. As he turned away from the woman, his hat still in hand, those eyes settled on Jake as if issuing a warning or statement of possessiveness. Jake let his eyes drop; he had no interest in the beauty, who was built along the lines of the portraits of undressed women one saw hanging behind the bar on saloon walls.

Jake's only interest was in wondering who she was, what she could possibly be doing in rough country like this. She was obviously no long-time resident of the area, not dressed like that! She seemed to Jake to be a woman waiting to go somewhere. But where? And what could she possibly have to do with this rough-country crowd?

2

By the flickering lantern light Jake finally got a clear look at the man who had called out his name in that vaguely familiar voice. He had taken off his hat as had his two partners, and his eyes emerged from the shadow of the brim. A small smile appeared on the pudgy face of Eric Grove as he realized that Jake now recognized the man who had been his cellmate for the first two months he had spent in Yuma Prison.

'Well, what do you know!' Jake said. He shook hands with Grove, but his eyes were still on the other two men — the handsome mustached one who believed he owned the statuesque brunette and the squat little one with the bugged-out eyes. Neither of them was smiling.

'I'll bet you never thought you'd see me again,' Eric Grove said. He inclined

21

his head toward a smaller room and Jake followed him in to a room where sat a desk and two facing black leather chairs. There was a mounted mule deer head on the wall, little else.

'Sit down,' Grove said, seating himself on a corner of the bare desk top. Fishing into his vest pocket he withdrew a cigar, offering it to Jake Worthy who shook his head negatively. Grove shrugged, lit a match with his thumbnail, drew in and blew out a plume of blue smoke and let his eyes settle on Jake.

'What in the world are you fellows doing way out here?' Jake asked.

'We've been mostly waiting — for a couple of men to show up. They haven't come.'

Jake had been on the dark side of the law, and knew enough not to ask more questions about their intentions. Instead he asked, 'How'd you happen to find me?'

Grove blew out another stream of tobacco smoke and explained, 'As I told you, we were waiting for a couple of the boys to show up, getting impatient about it. Didn't know if they'd gotten themselves arrested along the way or pinned down by the Apaches somewhere. We heard some shots fired just over the hill and decided we'd better look into things. We saw you down on the ground, forted up beside your horse.

'Bill Davenport said to let it be, it was your business and none of ours.'

'Which one's he?' Jake enquired.

'The tall one with the thin mustache. The other's Sparky Finnet.' Blowing smoke toward the ceiling again, Grove went on, 'Anyway, I thought you looked familiar somehow. I told Davenport, 'Let's see how this plays out'. There wasn't much more to see, though. Whoever it was that shot you was long gone. Didn't see man, horse or even a swirl of dust anywhere around. When you finally got up from behind your horse, I recognized you even from that distance. We spent two months living together, after all.'

'Are you sure it wasn't you three who were shooting at me?' Jake asked. Eric Grove's normally affable expression hardened. His eyes narrowed.

'Now why in hell would we do that?' he asked. 'We're trying to hide out here quietly for a while, just until we get all the boys together. For all we knew there might have been a dozen men behind you on the trail. We sure didn't wish to announce our presence.'

'All right,' Jake said, holding up one hand, palm forward. 'I didn't mean to rile you. It's just that I have no idea who else it might have been — could have been.'

'I can't help you there,' Grove said. 'All I can figure is that whoever it was, he spotted the three of us up there before he could finish his business with you and took off.'

'That must have been the way it was,' Jake Worthy said. He wondered, 'How long have you men been up here; how much longer will you be staying?'

'We've been here a week, and we're cutting things close. Next day or two we're going to have to trail out whether the Macklin brothers show up or not.'

'That's who you're waiting for?'

'Those two — anything could have happened along the way. They might have gotten arrested trying to rob a candy store, maybe they decided to get good and drunk and stay that way — maybe their scalps are decorating an Apache lance.'

There was one other thing Jake was dying to ask about but, as he opened his mouth, Eric Grove spoke first cautioning him, 'Don't ask any questions about the woman. Yvonne Blaine is her name, that's all I'll say.'

'She sure doesn't look like she belongs here.'

'Who does!' Grove grinned. 'Godforsaken place, ain't it? Bill Davenport learned about it somehow and thought it would make a decent hideout. The story is that an old man found himself a little seam of gold up here and decided he was going to stay and work it, Apaches or not. Built himself this place which could hold off an army attack. Then, of course, the Indians got him anyway. A man can't stay holed up all day long and get his mining work done too.'

Jake was aware of movement behind him, but he did not turn his head. Grove's eyes flickered that way and he said, 'Howdy, Bill.'

'You two finished talking over old times?' Bill Davenport asked.

'Just about,' Grove said with a nod. He was putting out his cigar in a large stone ashtray which might have once been an Indian *metate* used for grinding corn, chia and other grains.

'Did you put it to him?' Davenport asked, still not approaching the two men.

'I figured that was your decision to make, not mine,' Grove said, with a smile meant to be ingratiating. 'You're the man in charge.'

'Yes,' Davenport said icily, 'I am.'

What was bothering Davenport? Having Grove find a man whom Davenport took to be his old trailmate, but who had in fact never seen Grove before or since the two months they spent together in prison?

'Sparky says he recognizes Worthy too,' Davenport told them.

Sparky? How was that possible? Jake was sure that he had never seen the little man with the frog eyes in prison or out. 'I don't believe I've ever met that man,' Jake said, now turning his head to study the tall, composed Davenport who stood watching him with dark, measuring eyes.

'I didn't say you've met,' Bill Davenport said with carefully measured words, 'I said he recognized you.' Jake frowned and shrugged.

'I don't get you.'

Now pacing the small room, Bill Davenport asked, 'Have you ever been to Tucson, Worthy?'

'Sure I have.'

Bill Davenport stopped his pacing

and stood looking up at the four-point mule deer head on the wall. The trophy was dusty. Its glass eyes looked at nothing. 'That's where Sparky hails from, you know. How about the Fairview Saloon, Worthy? Ever hear of such a place? Ever visited it?'

'Yes,' Jake admitted, 'I have.' *That was where all of his troubles had begun.*

'That's where Sparky recognizes you from. You drew a lot of attention to yourself one night. Shot a gambler named Ned Quirk over a false deal. Sparky says he was watching and that you are lightning fast with a gun and a true shot even when you're off-balance and falling.'

'That was pretty much luck and instinct,' Jake Worthy told him.

'That's pretty much what all gun fighting is, isn't it?' Davenport asked, taking two steps toward Jake.

'I suppose so. Look, Davenport, if there's a point to all of this, I'd appreciate it if you'd just get to it.' Jake's wounded leg was beginning to stiffen up on him, and he stretched it out in front of him a few times while Davenport watched, framing a response.

'Did Grove tell you anything about our business?' he asked, glancing at Eric Grove who seemed to shrink a little under that gaze.

'No,' Jake said flatly, trying to protect his old cellmate who might have said more than he meant to.

'No matter,' Davenport said, waving a hand in the air. 'Who are you going to tell anyway?'

Jake was silent, not liking the way things seemed to be developing. Grove had moved away from the desk and now Davenport took a seat on it, facing Jake Worthy.

'We're short on men for a little adventure we've got planned. The thing is, we don't have the time to wait any longer for the boys who were supposed to be riding with us. How'd you like a job, Worthy?'

'Not much,' Jake replied immediately.

'I've lost my horse, I have a hole in my leg. I just got out of prison. I was on my way to meet my sweetheart in Rio Lobo.'

'That's all in the past, isn't it?' Davenport said. He was smiling, but it was not a friendly expression. 'We could send you on your way right now, let you have the cold desert. I'd give you hundred to one odds you'd never make it to Rio Lobo. What do you think?'

'I think you're probably right,' Jake said unhappily.

'On the other hand if you stick with us, I'll see that you get a horse, your guns and some generous pocket money to carry with you when you get back home to see that girl.'

Jake listened and nodded. His leg was really bothering him and he told Davenport so. 'Let me sleep overnight and think about it.'

'I'll give you that long,' Davenport said, 'No longer. You can make up your mind — ride out with us or try to walk out on your own.'

There was no choice. Jake nodded his head wearily. His leg had begun to burn again and his head ached like the devil. Unspeaking, Eric Grove guided Jake down the hallway of the stone house to a tiny room with a cot and a chair, a bedside table in it, nothing else.

As Jake struggled to remove his boots, Grove said, 'I'm sorry, Jake, but you see how it is. Besides, it won't be too bad. Soon you'll be riding home to your woman with a pocket full of gold.'

Jake only nodded again. The effort it took to get his boots off was Herculean. Removing his trousers was not much easier. He lay back on the cot, letting his head drop against the thin pillow. Sleep would not come, but it made no difference. He would have been awakened anyway by the specter who showed herself in the doorway carrying a lantern. Yvonne placed the lamp and a metal tray on the bedside table.

'I've come to see to you,' she said in a throaty voice.

Davenport arrived before she could

seat herself, his face furious. 'Just what do you think you're doing, Yvonne?'

'Just what you might think,' she answered calmly, no expression passing across her face. 'We're asking this man to ride with us to Belmont and he's badly wounded. He's of no use if he dies along the way.'

So saying, she flipped the blanket away from Jake's leg and examined the wound which was now encrusted with dried blood, the flesh around it inflamed. Davenport had come nearer to peer over her shoulder.

'I don't like you doing this,' he said in a menacing voice, his eyes fixed on Jake Worthy.

Yvonne did not react except to say in the same calm voice, 'I've seen a leg before. You want him well enough to be able to ride with us, don't you? Leave me alone.'

Reluctantly, angrily, Bill Davenport stamped out the door and down the hall.

'He's such a stupid man,' Yvonne

said softly as she washed the scab away from Jake's wound with cloth and warm water. 'And he thinks too highly of himself.' She did not look at Jake's face as she murmured these words.

'Now,' Yvonne announced, 'I am going to hurt you, Mr Worthy.'

With that dire announcement, she picked up two items from the metal tray she had brought with her. Jake recognized the green bottle which contained carbolic. It was used on the range from everything to cleaning castrated steers to treating bullet wounds. She splashed this freely on a ball of linen which was attached to a long dowel that looked like it had been the handle of a wooden kitchen spoon.

'My leg's healing well enough on its own,' Jake said with trepidation.

'No, it's not. it's scabbing over, but what's inside?' Looking again at the bullet hole which went from side to side through the meaty part of his thigh, she announced, 'This must be done.' She was expressionless. Jake realized that he had never seen a flicker of emotion on the dark woman's beautiful face. She was as cool as an ice maiden. Her eyes, however, were intent.

She asked him, 'This was a .44-40, wasn't it?'

'I think so.'

She examined the diameter of the wooden rod she held, and nodded. 'Almost the same,' she said. Then without further preparation she poked the rod with its carbolic-drenched linen head into the bullet hole. Jake almost blacked out. His hands were clenched tightly. The pain was incredible as she methodically prodded and twisted the dowel through his leg muscle. It hurt worse than being shot had. There was no expression on Yvonne's businesslike face, certainly no pity. She resembled some medical student practicing on a corpse.

Jake glanced down and saw the carbolic-soaked linen head now bloody, emerge from the exit wound. Yvonne snatched the linen away from the dowel's head and nodded as if in satisfaction. Then she did glance at Jake whose face was pale with pain.

'That was the worst part,' she said and then gave a terrific yank on the probe and withdrew it in one swift stoke. Again Jake felt his world whirl, again he almost fainted. He found that he was panting. If that was the cure, it had been worse than the cause.

Yvonne said, 'That should kill any infection. Now we won't have to think about taking your leg off.'

This, too, was delivered in a thoughtful, matter-of-fact tone of voice. Jake moaned a little despite his best efforts. He heard the implements clattering back into the tray, and lifted his head weakly, feeling that he should say something to the woman, but she was already slipping out of the room, unperturbed, neither smiling nor scowling, just a tall, mysterious mountain phantom.

Jake was sure he would not sleep on this night after that, but as the moon rose higher, visible only through the slit window in his room, he did. It was not the deep, untroubled rest he would have preferred, but it was all that could have been expected.

Considering he had been shot, threatened, roughly treated, made an enemy of a jealous man and commanded to take part in some crooked scheme or face death on the long desert, it was amazing that he was able to sleep at all.

Lord knew what daylight might bring. Jake could not envision things getting much better, but he could see that they might get a lot worse.

3

Morning was a single piercing ray of light through the slit window of the stone wall. It reminded Jake of the throttled dawns that arrived, almost unnoticed, in prison. Those faint glimmers that brought no bright hope, but only the certainty that some unwanted, forced labor lay ahead. Jake lay abed as long as possible, knowing that his sense of freedom was an illusion. He was unwilling to rise and face the new day with its false promise.

Eric Grove, smiling without conviction, arrived in the doorway within an hour.

'Time to go, Jake. We've miles to ride, and time's a-wasting.'

'What's the rush?' Jake Worthy asked, levering himself to a seated position.

'Somebody will explain along the way. For now, Bill Davenport wants everyone fed and mounted before the sun heats up.'

Jake only nodded. What was there to discuss? He went along with them or was left here, injured and without a horse.

After a breakfast which was corn pone, bacon and coffee — apparently all they had left to eat — Jake Worthy was instructed by Davenport to go outside. Everyone had left his dishes on the table. Well, why not, they were never coming back?

The sun was a low ball of light to the east lifting itself from the long desert horizon. It was still cool in the yard in front of the stone house when Grove and Sparky Finnet arrived with their horses. Jake had seen no corral the night before, but there must have been one behind the house. Yvonne appeared in the doorway, her dark hair brushed to a gloss, loosely arranged at the back of her sleek neck. She wore a white, long-sleeved blouse, tan twill jodhpurs and ox-blood half boots. He waited, expecting her to emerge with a trunk or at least a suitcase, but the woman was apparently ready to ride. He asked Eric Grove about it quietly.

'She'll have an entire new wardrobe after we finish the job,' Grove replied. 'She'll be able to afford anything she needs.'

Grove sounded confident; everyone acted confident — except Jake Worthy who as yet had no idea what he had gotten himself into.

He was given an aged black and white paint pony which had its best years behind it. There was no way he was going to escape the gang on this horse, but it was a comfort to be back in the saddle again once he was able to climb aboard. Now would Davenport let him have his guns back? Not likely, it seemed. Jake recognized his own gunbelt, its Colt in its holster, riding on the pommel of Davenport's saddle cinched down on his horse, a tall, strapping blue roan.

Before Jake was fully settled into

leather, they began riding out, following a twisting, stony trail down the gray hills toward the white desert, the low sun bright in the pale sky. Jake had his hat tipped low as did the others as they made their way though a ragged stand of greasewood and started out on to the desert flats, their shadows stretched out behind them.

Bill Davenport and Yvonne, on a leggy sorrel, rode ahead of them, Davenport trying to speak to the woman who ignored him, either out of dislike or habit. Her eyes were fixed only on the horizon. After them rode Jake Worthy and Eric Grove. Behind, Sparky Finnet rode at a little distance, his rifle across his saddlebow. His frog eyes were fixed on Jake, as if wishing he would try to make a break for it.

Which would have been a wild-eyed idea, with a slow pony, no weapon and a wounded leg and nowhere to run. Still Finnet's glare did not falter. 'I don't think the man likes me,' Jake muttered, and Eric Grove heard him.

'Hell, it's not that, Jake,' Grove said lightly. 'You see how it is. They don't know you, and they're counting on your help. You should have sounded more eager to make some money.'

'Should I have? I don't know if I am or not, to tell you the truth. I'd much rather be riding alone and free, heading back to Rio Lobo.'

'Well,' Grove said, 'there you have it. Don't you think that they know that?'

Jake had no answer to that remark. He rode on, under a high sun which was gradually going white to match the desert salt flats. He noticed that Davenport had given up trying to talk to the woman. His face was angry, frustrated. It was obvious that Davenport was wanting to claim Yvonne for his own; just as obvious that he was being rejected at the moment. Jake Worthy wished someone would tell him what was going on, but, as the sun rose higher and beat down on their backs, shoulders and necks, no one spoke at all.

It was hell out there by noon. There were heat veils rising ahead of them, obscuring the land. Davenport called a brief halt and they all drank from their canteens. The water was tepid, but welcome.

When they started on again, Jake was surprised to see Erie Grove go to the point to ride alongside Yvonne while Davenport held back his pony to take up a position nearer to Jake Worthy. The two men spoke as they rode.

'You'll find out soon enough anyway,' Bill Davenport said, his black eyes hidden in the shadow of his hat brim, 'so it's time you found out what's going on.'

'I'd appreciate it,' Jake said a little roughly. The elderly paint horse they had provided him with was stumbling beneath him and Jake had to keep lifting its head with the reins. He couldn't tell for sure, but it seemed the old-timer was constantly threatening to go to sleep beneath him, rather than succumbing to simple weariness.

'I know you've been in a few scrapes in your time, Worthy; Grove has told me.'

'Here and there,' Jake admitted. He regretted those years, but it was true. After being released from prison this time, he had sworn never to fall into anything like that again. He only wanted to settle down with Becky Holland, if she would still have him.

'Anyway,' Davenport said, 'this is the way things are planned: there's a certain freight office in Belmont that has been holding a lot of money for the mines' payrolls there. Well, tomorrow is payday, which is why we couldn't wait any longer for the Macklin brothers — whatever might have become of them.'

'Why the freight office and not the bank?' Jake asked reasonably. Davenport laughed out loud.

'The freight office has a massive Coventry safe with walls of three-inch thick steel. The bank has a tin box.'

'I see. Tell me, is one of you a safe

cracker or are you just going to blow the thing up?'

Davenport leaned toward him. 'Neither, Worthy — we've got the combination to that big old safe.'

'But how . . . ?'

'You see that girl riding up there?' Davenport asked smugly. 'Her father owns the freight office. She was looking around for some help and I met up with her. I told her I could put a gang together in no time — which I almost did. Except for the damned Macklins . . . '

'How many men were you planning on using, the five of you?'

'With the Macklin brothers it should have been five, yes. One man posted around the back to watch the rear door. Two of us to walk inside and take care of anyone there. One posted outside the front to stand guard, and one just to hold the ponies so we wouldn't have to tie up. I saw a man robbing a bank down in Apache Wells once. He would have got away clean. He had the money in his hands. He couldn't get his horse untied from the hitch rail and they caught up with him before he could ride out.'

Jake Worthy nodded. He had heard such tales before. 'What's my job supposed to be?'

'You'll be taking two jobs. I want you guarding the front entrance while Grove and I go inside. You'll have to hold the horses at the same time — but then you can shoot with one hand, can't you?' Davenport chuckled.

'After Grove and I have secured the place and put whoever's there face down on the floor, Yvonne will make her entrance, walk to the safe and simply spin the dial on that big Coventry.'

'She doesn't mind robbing her own father?' Jake asked.

'She's eager to,' Davenport said. 'Then me and her are heading out for the far country, maybe Mexico. You and the boys can head wherever you like — with you I guess it's back to Rio Lobo.'

'I suppose,' Jake said with little enthusiasm. He had been studying his belt gun which still dangled from Davenport's saddle horn. 'I'll be needing that,' he said, nodding at the holstered Colt.

Davenport looked down. 'Of course you will,' he agreed, 'when it's time.'

By mid-afternoon they had crested a line of low hills where grass struggled to grow, and they looked down on the town of Belmont. It was a prettier town than most Jake had run across out here — a church with a steeple, four or five red-brick buildings in the center of town and many white clapboard structures with only a few poor adobes scattered along the outlying roads. Here and there stood dusty live oaks and a few sycamore trees, and he could see a narrow rill, flashing silver in the late sunlight: the source of the town's life.

'Which one is the freight office?' Jake asked of Eric Grove who had halted beside him on the knoll.

'See that green building just off the

main street?' Grove pointed. 'I guess that's it, from what they've told me.'

'You've never been here before?' Jake enquired. Grove shook his head.

'No, and I don't expect I ever will come here again — not after this.'

'What's Davenport waiting for? Are we going down today?'

'I believe so. I think he's just resting the horses. We might need fresh mounts under us after we've made our move.'

Jake nodded mutely. No amount of rest was going to lend the grandfather of a paint pony he was mounted on any more speed. The old boy just didn't have it anymore. He would be left far behind if they had to make a dash for it. Not that it would bother Davenport or any of the others if he lagged and was captured.

And likely hanged.

Davenport walked his horse nearer and spoke to the group. 'Let's take different routes into town. No point in moving in a body — it might alert someone. You and Worthy,' he said to

Grove, 'ride in from the east end and make your way to the freight office. Everybody should know by now what his job is once we get there.'

'I still don't have a pistol,' Jake said, but Davenport had already turned his blue roan away from them and started down the trail to the west of town, Yvonne at his side, Sparky Finnet trailing after them. 'What in hell am I supposed to do if someone spots us?' Jake asked unhappily.

'Yell as loud as you can,' Grove said and, damn him, he was smiling.

It was obvious to Jake now that he was not going to be trusted to do anything but hold the horses out front. Maybe it was for the best, he considered. He had no wish to go to shooting. Still, it irked him. Probably Davenport did not wish him armed until the loot, if it was taken at all, was divided to his own liking. Jake was, after all, not a member of the gang, but only an emergency replacement. He found himself cursing the missing Macklin brothers as he followed Eric Grove down the slope toward the town of Belmont. Why couldn't they have kept their appointment? Of course, if they had, the gang might have decided to simply leave Jake alone on the desolate hillside where he had been shot, having no concern about him and no possible use for a wounded man.

It didn't matter now. Willingly or not, Jake was in this up to his neck and with no way out.

He and a grim-faced Eric Grove entered the town at its eastern head and quickly veered toward a parallel alley where their progress could not be seen by prying eyes. Reaching the street where the green freight office stood, Grove stopped for a minute, gesturing to Jake to stay back. Jake thought that the others must have been slower in reaching their destination, but then he spotted Davenport and Yvonne in the alley across the way, Davenport holding the reins to Finnet's horse. They were simply giving Sparky time to post himself at the rear door of the building.

All was ready then. Jake rode forward with Eric Grove, crossing the dusty street to where Davenport and Yvonne waited. Jake's mouth was dry, his heart racing. He had been in situations like this before, but he had never liked the feeling he had when the job was about to come off. Without a gun at hand he liked it even less.

One by one the other three swung down from their mounts and handed the leathers to Jake who could do nothing but stand watching for men approaching the freight office. Jake saw Davenport take a deep breath and nod to Eric Grove. Both had their pistols in their hands as they entered the building. Yvonne stood to one side of the door, clutching a green canvas bag, her face revealing neither excitement nor fear.

No one moved along the street. From inside Jake heard a scuffling sound and something clattering to the floor. Then all was silent and Yvonne swept through the door as if she were an uninterested observer.

It was two or three minutes later, no more, that a gun's report sounded inside. The horses backed away nervously. Yvonne's sorrel reared up and Jake fought to control the animals as his eyes swept the street, expecting men to come looking, perhaps even a charge of townsmen led by men with badges. He needed his gun now, damn Davenport! But the shot seemed to have aroused no curiosity around the area. Perhaps because the freight office was located off the main street, or, possibly, sheer indifference of the citizens of Belmont to a single muffled shot having been fired.

But who had fired the shot, and who had been hit?

Seconds later, Yvonne backed out of the freight office, a pistol in one hand, the green satchel in the other. Jake expected the others to burst out through the doorway, but no one else appeared. Yvonne approached Jake with those long strides of hers, her face expressionless as she grabbed the reins to her sorrel from Jake's hand and told him, 'Swing up! We're riding.' When Jake hesitated she waved the Colt revolver she was carrying — his own — in his direction.

'What about — ?'

'Let's get going — now!'

Anything to oblige a lady. He mounted the paint pony and followed Yvonne down the alley, riding at a rapid trot to keep up with her. The paint didn't care for it. As they reached a grove of cottonwood trees which stood beyond the town limits, Yvonne held up her sorrel and ordered Jake, 'Get rid of that clomping beast. Ride Davenport's blue. It's got speed.'

As Jake switched horses, cutting the paint horse loose to wander, Yvonne went on, 'We need to keep moving, and fast. There are other horses in that town, you know, and Bill Davenport won't waste time purchasing them. They could already be into leather.

Hurry up, will you!'

Impatient, Yvonne spurred her horse forward, Jake Worthy following her through the brief shade of the cotton-wood grove out on to open land beyond, leading Eric Grove and Fin-net's animals.

They met the silver rill Jake had seen from the knoll above the town and Yvonne paused long enough for Jake to ask, 'Which way?'

'Do you know this country?' she asked coolly.

'No.'

'Then just follow me and keep an eye on the back-trail. You can let those spare ponies go now.' Was there any other choice? Yvonne led the way up and down rocky ridges, through hollows and up sandy bluffs. Jake had forgotten that Yvonne had grown up in Belmont and had probably ridden the trails she was following dozens of times.

At length Yvonne drew her horse up in the shade of a pair of wide-spreading oak trees which stood on a knoll stained with yellow grass. Bill Davenport's blue roan was not even laboring for breath. Outlaws bought the finest horses they could find just for this reason. There might have been a posse behind them, and certainly Davenport and his men would try to follow, but there was little chance of catching up with Jake and Yvonne considering the pace they had set, the circuitous path she had chosen. Any horsemen following would be forced to search for their sign constantly and were bound to fall far behind as the escaping pair rode on at full speed.

Or so Jake hoped. When Yvonne again set off, Jake was able to match the stride of the blue roan to that of her horse.

'Do you mind telling me where we're going . . . and what happened back there?'

'What happened?' Yvonne said, frowning with her eyebrows as if it were a stupid question. 'I robbed my father's freight office. Twisted the dial on the safe and the money nearly tumbled out into my bag.'

'I know that much,' Jake said, in a sarcastic tone, as they reached a green grass valley and headed south. No livestock or structures were visible for miles around. 'That doesn't explain much.'

To Yvonne, who knew all that had transpired, this also seemed to be an unintelligent remark. She began to explain matters carefully and slowly as if speaking to a slightly slow child. The long, grassy valley was beginning to fade, their travel leading them toward a rocky, broken line of hills beyond. The sun was still bright and warm in a high sky, but the air around them was cooler, much cooler than the open desert they had crossed that morning.

Yvonne answered, but on a different, if related, subject.

'My father, Samuel Blaine, sent me to a fine, quite strict school back East when I was twelve — not for my benefit, but because he had promised my mother that he would. When my mother died, I came back to Belmont for the funeral, meaning to stay for a few days and then return East. I had gotten to like it back there — the dances, the fine clothes and clever young men, and here I was stuck in this little Podunk town of Belmont again, where the idea of a fancy dress is an old gingham one, and the most interesting thing the men do is drink beer and belch.

'I begged my father to let me have enough money to return to school, but he said he reckoned I'd had enough book-learning, and, besides, I had too many high-falutin' ideas for his taste already. I pleaded, I begged, I cajoled; it was as if he didn't even hear me. His promise to my mother seemed to have come to an end with her funeral.'

'You began to grow angry — and to scheme,' Jake suggested.

'Oh, did I get angry,' Yvonne answered. 'But that did me no good at all. Then, as you've said, I began to

56

scheme — in earnest.'

Jake only nodded. The land ahead began to rise and grow hard and menacing in the late afternoon light. Reddish slabs of rock tilted and jumbled into one another, outcrops appearing in unlikely places, maniacally formed, shuffled and dealt out haphazardly by some devious entity.

Jake let Yvonne lead the way. The trail grew steeper, wending its way upward through patches of reddish, reflected sunlight and deep shadows. He trusted Yvonne to lead the way, but he thought that would be the only thing he could trust her on. When the trail widened to allow it, Jake pulled up beside her again, wanting to get the rest of the story — after all, their fates were now intertwined.

Yvonne said with an exaggerated sigh, 'I went looking for a partner. Bill Davenport was the first available ally I ran across. I don't know his background, but I know it was unsavory. And he was greedy.'

'And he liked you,' Jake pointed out. Yvonne looked for a moment as if she might actually smile. She did not.

'Do you know how easy it is for a woman to get a man to want her?'

'I have an idea.'

'And, as I say, he was greedy. All thieves are greedy. They want as much as they can take with the least possible amount of effort. When I told him I had the combination to the freight office's safe, he was easily hooked. Except, he said, we needed to gather a few more men. It wouldn't do for him to walk in and hold a gun on the clerks while I twirled the safe's lock. If my father, another worker, or the law caught us at it, we would have had no chance.'

'So he recruited Eric Grove, Sparky Finnet and the Macklin brothers.'

'Yes — I didn't like dividing the money so many ways, but from the sly little remarks Bill made, I don't think he ever intended to split it with all of them anyway,' Yvonne went on. 'Then something happened to the Macklin brothers, leaving us two men short. They found you, and Eric Grove immediately told Bill that you were a natural fill-in: a gunhand and a former prisoner. There was little choice. Bill decided he had better take the chance with you. Not that he trusted you much.'

'So I noticed,' Jake Worthy grunted, as he forced the blue up a rocky step in the road. Bill Davenport's pony was a strong runner, and swift, but he had no liking for rough country.

'Nor did I trust Bill Davenport,' Yvonne said, 'So, I decided to take matters into my own hands.'

4

As they approached the crest of the rocky trail, Jake following Yvonne upward, Jake heard a small splat and saw the blue roan he was riding toss its head in irritation as if a horse fly had bitten it. But it was no horse fly. A moment later the dull echo of a distant shot sounded and Jake, examining the ear of the roan, saw the hole neatly punched through it. Yvonne had not reacted or had failed to connect the sound with what had happened, but Jake urged her on more quickly, swatting the flank of her sorrel with the ends of his reins.

Yvonne fixed an angry glare on him, but lifted her horse to a quicker pace until they were up and over the ridge as purple twilight began to settle across the rugged land. Without speaking, Jake showed Yvonne the bullet hole in the roan's ear as they drew up at a bend in the trail. Whoever had fired the rifle was a damned good shot, and the bullet had passed within inches of Jake's head.

'I don't think they're ready to give it up,' Jake said tightly.

'No,' she agreed, 'it seems not.' But her voice had no fear in it, her face revealed no panic.

'Look, Yvonne . . . ' Jake said to the ice maiden, but she was not listening. She had opened the green satchel where the stolen money was held. From the bag she removed Jake's Colt and gunbelt. She passed it over to him as the horses stood catching their breath, the roan still shaking its head.

'It's time you started carrying this again,' she said, then led the way down the far side of the ridge, her manner calm and precise. Jake hastily strapped on his gun and caught up with her as she began crossing a narrow high-country valley.

'How long have you known Eric Grove?' she asked, barely glancing at him. 'I know he's your friend.'

'You have to be friends with someone you're locked in with for twenty-four hours a day. Otherwise things get ugly.'

'I understand,' Yvonne commented, although she could not possibly know without having been in the same circumstance. Jake was relaxing a little now, although he glanced back along the trail from time to time. Whoever it was who fired that shot had aimed it from a great distance, perhaps as much as a mile, and was still far behind, but he had proven that he could cause trouble even at that range.

'What was he like — Eric Grove?' Yvonne wanted to know. Maybe she was concerned that Jake and Grove might have a closer connection than she was aware of.

'I don't know, really. He was serving the last two months of his sentence while I was serving the first two of mine. He talked a lot. Had a lot of tall tales to spin — at least some of them must have been true or he wouldn't have ended up where he was.'

'But you two made no plans?'

'Plans?' Jake laughed. 'He was on his way out and I was set to do a long stretch. What plans could we make?'

'I don't know; criminals do, don't they? Plan their next big job?'

'Not me,' Jake answered. 'My only plan was to stay out of trouble and settle down with a nice little woman I know named Becky Holland over in Rio Lobo, if she'd have me.'

'Will she?' Yvonne asked. 'Have you?'

'I don't know — I've disappointed her a lot, and now I'm doing it again.'

'You just want to cut and run, then, is that right?'

'That's right,' Jake told her.

'Too bad you can't — not just yet,' Yvonne said. Halting her horse in the middle of the valley as the sky darkened she looked at him directly. Jake was puzzled and his face showed it. 'Is there a telegraph office in Rio Lobo?' she wanted to know.

'Yes. The wire was run in a little over

a year ago. Why?'

'Just wondered,' Yvonne said, and started on again, but Jake grabbed the bridle of her sorrel and demanded, 'Why did you ask that, Yvonne?'

'I was just thinking about what might happen if you ran out on me, now when I need you the most. Those men back there,' she said tossing her head, 'they might catch up, you know. If that happens I want a man who's good with a gun riding with me.'

'And if I choose not to be that man?'

Yvonne shrugged with one shoulder. She was still unsmiling as she answered. 'Well, then, Jake Worthy, you would find yourself in a lot of trouble. You were a participant in a freight-office robbery, you're riding a stolen horse, and . . . you're a kidnapper. That would be the story that I'd have telegraphed to Rio Lobo. They'd arrest you on sight — and two of those charges are hanging offenses.'

Jake was seething because he knew the woman was capable of doing just what she was threatening and that to anyone who didn't know the facts, the story would have the ring of truth. Here he was, the public would imagine, armed and dangerous, forcing a young woman across the country with a satchel full of stolen money, riding a stolen horse. And he knew that Yvonne could be counted on to make an excellent witness for the prosecution. If matters ever came to that point, she could count on her father's support, and she would get away with it scot-free, ready to go home and make a new play or simply convince her father that this was why she wanted to return East to school — things were just too wild out in this part of the country.

The lady held all the cards and Jake knew it. He fell in with her, riding the trail toward their unknown destination. Her reluctant bodyguard. He did wonder: 'What happened back in Belmont, Yvonne? You never told me.'

'It was simple,' she said without either pride or apparent shame. 'Only

Chris Gore and Jack Halley, his assistant, were supposed to be working in the office, but there might have been customers, people dropping by, so Davenport and Eric Grove went in with guns drawn and ordered the two clerks to the floor. Then I went in.

'The safe was nothing — I'd opened it a dozen times before. I filled the satchel and turned around with my own pistol — your pistol — leveled. I told Davenport and Grove to drop their guns and hit the floor as well. Davenport hesitated, smiling as if he took it for a joke. So I fired the pistol off into the ceiling and both of them went down to kiss wood.

'Sparky Finnet who was outside the back door rushed in and I waved the gun his way. I told him to lose his pistol and get down too. He complied. He didn't see any smile on my face. Just a Colt trickling smoke in my hand. You know the rest,' she concluded.

Her expression was brazen, confident as they continued on through the near-darkness. The first stars were already visible to the east. No one, Jake decided, could follow their trail now that daylight was gone. Unless someone guessed their destination.

'Where are we headed?' Jake Worthy asked.

'Robles, it's called,' Yvonne answered, without turning her head.

'A town?'

'Not really. It's just a collection of sheep farmers. They've lived out here for years and years.'

'They know you there, do they?'

'They did. I haven't been out here since I was twelve or thirteen years old. They were hospitable to me, friendly as people tend to be in these remote settlements who seldom see visitors.'

Jake nodded. He followed the woman through the dimness, hoping that she was right. She seemed to have taken a lot of time to plan out her escape, but there's always something that can go wrong with any plan. Ahead now he thought he saw a thin spiral of blue smoke rising against the dark sky, and he could smell wood burning. Half a mile on he saw a few scattered, tiny structures. Through one window he could see firelight. They had come upon Robles.

A trio of black and white sheepdogs came out barking at them, then positioned themselves behind the horses as if meaning to drive the animals into the sheep pens which were crowded with wooly white bodies.

Visible in the gloom of the evening were four or five adobe houses, small and square with flat roofs, along with a series of smaller outbuildings the roofs of which were formed of stacks of bound and interlaced brush. It didn't look like much, but apparently served the purpose. Yvonne rode directly toward one of the huts. Jake followed uncertainly, his eyes still going frequently toward the back trail. They might have temporarily lost their pursuers, but Davenport and his crew would not give up easily, and daylight would find the outlaws mounted again.

Eric Gore would continue because he had started the job, and would want to see it through — Jake knew him that well. The frog, Sparky Finnet, had no brain, or a very limited one, but he would follow Bill Davenport anywhere he asked him to. Besides, neither of the henchmen had received the pay they had been promised.

Davenport had no conscience, but he had a strong sense of pride. If word ever got around that he had been robbed at gun point by a woman who had then taken off with another man, he would be mocked unmercifully. The injury at the hands of a woman he had wanted, the insult of being rejected by her even as she made off with the proceeds from the hold up would be galling if he did not revenge himself. On top of losing the money, his manhood would have been wounded. Bill Davenport would not stand for that. There would be jeers or whispered words, muffled laughter wherever he went at least in his imagination.

No, Davenport would never give up.

And the law? Jake did not know what kind of law they had in Belmont, but he knew that Yvonne's father was a substantial citizen there. And the money, being held for the few scattered mines in the area, would be sorely missed by the mine owners and the men expecting their pay — it would be no problem to raise a sizeable posse.

Yvonne and Jake had not even begun to see the sort of uproar they had stirred up. Knowing Yvonne, she certainly had a plan in place to escape. Jake, who had been dragged into this at the last minute, had only a bleak vision of himself riding the land forever, trying to escape capture and the hangman's noose.

When they were within a hundred feet of the house Yvonne had been aiming for, the front door was swung open, and a man stepped out on to the low porch, summoned by the barking of the dogs.

'*Que es?*' he called. He had no gun in his hands, but there undoubtedly would be one near to hand.

'Domingo!' Yvonne called back cheerfully, still riding her horse forward at a walk. The man frowned, squinted into the night and then grinned broadly.

'Yvonne!' he shouted with surprise and apparent pleasure. Yvonne must have changed considerably since she had been a thirteen-year-old girl, but the man obviously recognized her, and he turned his head back toward the interior of the house, calling for others to come forth to greet her.

'Looks like you made an impression,' Jake commented. Yvonne did not answer. She took it as her due that she always made a considerable impression wherever she went. Probably, he reflected, she did.

He swung down and tied both horses to the hitch rail and stood by, watching as a swarm of happy-faced people from the grandfatherly Domingo to little children, well-rounded women in striped skirts, all gathered around Yvonne speaking half in Spanish, half in English. Yvonne was escorted into the little house, and after taking a minute to again examine their back trail, Jake Worthy followed.

His leg had stiffened after spending all day in the saddle and he limped a bit as he stepped inside the tiny, warm adobe hut. Yvonne had been seated in a leather-backed chair. People congregated around her as if she were some returning queen.

What could she ever have done for these people? Even as Jake pondered that, he saw Yvonne's hand dip into the green satchel and pass Domingo a stack of once-folded currency. Of course — her father was a wealthy man; she must once have helped these people with an infusion of cash money that made their harsh lives a little easier.

Almost immediately the women began

buzzing about in the adjoining kitchen, stirring pots and rattling dishes and they were served hot spicy food at a small, rough-hewn table. After the meal Yvonne claimed to be weary. A young boy was sent to lead the *caballos* to the horse corral. Jake and Yvonne were shown to two tiny side-by-side rooms with straw-stuffed mattresses positioned on rough-made beds. All of the furniture in the house was homemade, Jake had noticed. The rooms were designed to accommodate children, Jake decided as he lay back on the undersized bed, the mattress's straw stuffing crackling under him.

The door was closed and Jake tried to sleep, tried to pretend that he was not a gunman on the run from the law with a satchel full of stolen money and a crazy woman bandit.

★   ★   ★

Morning arrived with a shaft of orange light through the window of his room and the clatter of doings in the front room. He dressed and limped that way.

Smiling women served Yvonne and Jake their breakfast. After they had eaten, Domingo had their horses brought around and after a series of casual hugs and insincere promises, Jake Worthy and Yvonne rode out of the pueblo, the little group on the porch behind them waving until they were lost in the distance.

'Well, that was nice,' Yvonne said, as they rode over a series of purplish hills toward the orange morning sun. 'Don't you think?'

'If you say so,' Jake grumbled.

'Wasn't it nice to have a bed to sleep on, food to eat?'

'Of course it was,' Jake said, 'but if I were on the run alone, the first thing I'd do is avoid any inhabited place where someone could point his finger down the trail I've taken.'

'Domingo would never do a thing like that,' Yvonne said coolly.

'No, but even knowing that we had been there would give the trackers a better chance of picking up our trail. Then there's the money you were flashing around. It might give someone an idea.'

'Domingo is an old friend,' Yvonne protested. There was just the faintest hint of concern in her dark eyes.

'Yes, and I know you wanted to thank him, but you should have taken him aside and just slipped the bills into his hand. There were a lot of people in the house, Yvonne. Even if someone didn't manage to peek into the satchel as you were giving the money to Domingo, they would have certainly guessed there was more in the bag.'

'I can't believe . . . ' Yvonne objected, then said in a more abject voice. 'I'm sorry; I'm still brand new at this outlaw game.' She glanced around. 'You surely can't believe — '

'I *know* so,' Jake, who had been constantly watching their back trail since Belmont, told her. 'If you look back you can see two horsemen riding

75

after us, and they're coming at a pretty good pace.'

'Bill must have found us,' Yvonne said, sounding rattled for the first time since Jake had met her.

He shook his head. 'It's not Davenport unless they took the time to change their clothes for some reason. Besides, I'd think he must still be lost in the hills. This is someone else.'

'Someone from Robles?'

'Can't be from anywhere else. Let's keep riding until we find a likely place.'

'A likely place?' Yvonne asked blankly.

'A place to hunker down and wait for them — we have to turn them back, Yvonne. Likely we will have to trade lead with them.'

'To trade . . . oh, I see. I'm starting to be glad that I hired you on for this, Jake.'

When was that? Jake wondered. She had not hired him on for anything. He had been foxed and then threatened into this. Nevertheless, he was going to have to keep the trailing men away. He was sure that someone in the pueblo had smelled money and now they meant to have it — take it out on the open land where no one would ever discover their crime. Jake had been among and around these sorts of men too long and too often not to have an idea what they had in mind.

'Veer off to the south,' Jake said after another fifteen minutes. He knew the following riders were closing ground, and they were not going to outrun them easily. Ahead a gray granite outcropping bulked against the landscape. A wedge-shaped boulder some thirty feet high and perhaps a hundred long, it appeared to have a trail leading into it, but Jake doubted there was a way out. It could be a trap, but it was less of a trap than trying to outrun the following men across the open land.

'What are you planning to do?' Yvonne asked with uncertainty.

'They'll try to box us in. Eager as they are, they'll probably overlook the fact that they're boxing themselves in as well. They hope to surprise us — I plan on surprising them.'

'You're going to kill them?' Yvonne asked. Her usual emotionless expression had returned,

Her voice was hard and seemed uncaring.

'I hope not to have to,' Jake replied, 'but I won't have them killing me either.'

The sun was still in their eyes, glinting off the mica in the walls of the granite monolith as they entered its dark corridor. As he had expected, Jake saw no way to pass through the rock. It didn't matter; he had never intended to continue running from the men behind them. He reminded himself that these were probably simple sheepherders acting on the spur of the moment, but that made them no less deadly. They would not wish to leave any witnesses to their crime in case the law were to come poking around one day.

'I wish I had my rifle,' Jake complained, as he swung down in the deep shade of the crevice and crouched there for a moment trying to revive his wounded leg.

'I can't help that,' Yvonne said defensively. 'It would hardly have fit in the satchel. Besides, you have your pistol, and you are a skilled gunfighter. That's why I hired you.'

Hired. That inapt word again. Jake knew that this 'reputation' he had of being a gunfighter of some sort derived from one lucky shot in Tucson, an event which Sparky Finnet had happened to witness, providing Jake with his bona fides. Jake was no better than many other men walking the West, certainly not as good as the best. He was not ashamed of what he could do with a handgun, but neither was it something to brag about.

'I want you to move toward the back of the crevice and just stay there,' Jake said, coming to his feet. 'I'm going to give these men one chance to back off and then it will be up to them. They're not professional thieves, I know that.

Maybe a warning will be enough.'

'I think I recognize one of them,' Yvonne said in a taut whisper, as the riders came nearer. 'The one on the bay horse — that's Domingo's nephew, Esteban. He was in the house last night when we came. The other man I don't know.'

'It doesn't matter who he is,' Jake said. 'We know his intent now, draw back as I told you, as far into the notch as you can get. Take my horse too.'

'What are you going to do?' Yvonne asked.

'I don't know yet,' Jake admitted. 'Just do what I say.'

As Yvonne faded into the deep shadows of the crevice, Jake searched for a position from where to brace the men. Twenty feet above the floor of the split rock, he spotted a ledge which might serve the purpose if he could find a way to clamber up. His leg, inconveniently, had decided to flare up again with pain.

This was a damnable business, Jake

thought, as he clawed his way up the rock face. There had been no good days, even hours, since he had met this woman, and everything was bound to get worse until he could find a way to get rid of her.

The granite face of the cleft crumbled beneath his fingers as he tried to make his way on to the low bench he had seen. At times he could find no toehold for his boots as he dragged and clawed his way upward. Reaching the narrow outcropping he lay on his stomach, trying to catch his breath. It was a bad spot in which he found himself, but still immeasurably better than remaining where he had been.

Lifting his head he saw the two horsemen as they entered the split rock and the shadows darkened their sun-bright silhouettes to shadowy images. The men drew their horses up, discussing matters. Their eyes were not yet adjusted to the shadows. Undoubtedly, being local men, they knew that there was no way to exit the rock's split except to ride past them. Confidently one of them — Esteban — drew his rifle from its scabbard and started his horse forward at a walk, his less-confident companion lagging behind him on a red roan. Jake couldn't let them get any closer. He lifted his voice, 'That's far enough, men. There's nothing in here for you except trouble and death.'

The two reined up their horses sharply and searched the shadows for the speaker. Jake's voice echoed weirdly across the interior of the monolith, and it was obvious that they could not discover his location by the bewildered expression on their young, dark faces.

'Go home!' Jake shouted, and then in case they hadn't understood his warning, he repeated it all in his broken, but intelligible Spanish. As he finished his warning, Esteban's eyes lit up and he lifted his rifle; he had managed to spot Jake on the ledge above them. Perhaps a ray of sunlight had reflected off some bit of metal Jake wore.

Esteban took aim but Jake, who had position and was more settled, triggered off with his Colt. Esteban's hands flew up into the air and his rifle fell free as his horse reared up. That should have been enough to deter the other rider, but he was determined, and before the echo of Jake's shot had faded away, the second rider had drawn his pistol.

He unleashed three .44 rounds from his revolver, pelting Jake Worthy with splinters of stone and rock dust, the bullets whining off into the distance. On his elbows, Jake took more careful aim than the robber on horseback had managed, and sighted, firing twice. The second round was unnecessary as the ill-fated thief tumbled from the saddle and lay still against the hard earth.

Yesterday morning at this time both of these men had been carefree sheep herders, Jake reflected. Then the scent of money had tempted them to their end. The story was old, but it seemed it was a constant one.

Sliding back down the rock face, Jake

hit the flat ground with a jolt he could feel from ankle to hip. His injured leg began to throb violently once again. He limped toward the two men lying on the ground, but there was nothing he could do for them — nothing anyone could have done.

Feeling a little like a vulture, Jake snatched up Esteban's Henry repeating rifle and stood staring down at the dead men. At the sound of approaching horses, Jake glanced toward the rear of the cleft to see Yvonne leading Davenport's blue roan, riding to meet him. Her face was calm as usual, her eyes expressionless as she viewed the bodies of the dead.

'I knew you could take care of them,' she said, flicking the reins of the blue roan to Jake. 'Let's get moving, shall we? There is still much to do if we are to be successful.'

5

They traveled on as the sun rose higher in the sky, heating the land which was low yellow grass and scattered live oak trees. Farther ahead Jake could see no vegetation of any kind, just rust-colored hills falling toward a narrow red earth valley. It seemed a good enough time to ask the lady:

'Where are we going, Yvonne? What's the plan now?'

'Once we clear this pass, we turn north again,' she answered. 'Just west of Bisbee there is a railroad watering stop. I mean to board the train there and travel East.'

'Resuming your former life.'

'Yes,' she said, and added a little wistfully, 'and don't you think there aren't people there who will be happy that I have returned.'

'A man?' Jake asked.

'All sorts of people,' she replied, 'but yes, a man, a man with breeding who knows how to dress and has the manners of a true gentleman.'

Jake shook his head. He wondered what that true gentleman would think of her if he knew what Yvonne had done on her visit to the West. He had a larger concern, however.

He asked Yvonne, 'What about me? What am I supposed to do? There's a lot of angry men searching for me.'

She shrugged, almost smiled and said, 'You're a hard man of the West, Jake Worthy. You've been in situations like this before. You know how to flee and how to hide.'

It was nice to know that the lady was so confident in his abilities to escape not only the vengeful Davenport gang, but the law and a rough bunch of angry citizens. Jake himself was not so certain. There was another matter that might prove helpful if he was forced to run. He broached the subject as they reached the foot of the pass and turned northward across the empty land.

'You keep saying that you hired me for protection: when do I get paid for the job?'

Their horses walked on, their hoofs crushing the dry yellow grass. 'I've been thinking about that,' Yvonne said casually. 'I've decided that you may have my horse.'

'Your horse?' Jake said.

'It's a fine animal,' Yvonne said, patting the sorrel's neck. 'You may need a second mount while escaping the men back there.' She shrugged again. 'When you no longer need it, it will bring a good price.'

'A fine partner you are,' Jake muttered.

'I never said we were partners,' Yvonne corrected him coolly.

'No, you didn't. Don't you see that taking your horse is more of a liability than a help? It will be proof that I have kidnapped you, as people — your father, especially — are bound to think. They'll assume that I've murdered you, hidden the cash and stolen your horse. The only ones who know the truth of the matter are members of Davenport's gang, and I doubt they'd step up to help me. It would only incriminate them; they wouldn't be believed anyway, you being the upstanding girl that you are.'

Yvonne was thoughtful. 'No,' she answered, 'I see what you mean, but I still think the sorrel is a fair payment for the amount of time you've spent.'

'You could at least buy me a ticket east on the railroad too. Maybe I could make my escape that way.'

'I wouldn't want to do that,' Yvonne said. 'That would put you too close to me. It's better if you just go your own way.' She halted her horse and studied him briefly. 'Or you could just rob me, murder me and get away with the money.'

'Murder you?' Jake asked in astonishment.

'You'd have to, wouldn't you? If you just let them find me, I'll tell them a series of lies which will be believed.'

'I could never kill you, any woman, any man without serious provocation. I'm not that type of man.'

'I know that,' Yvonne said, with a hint of triumph in her voice. 'That's why I selected you for the job.'

She was crazy, Jake told himself, as they started their horses on again. Not lock-her-up-and-throw-away-the-key-mad, but mad all the same. She lived in a different world than other people. Only her own needs and desires concerned her. There was nothing to be done with such a woman. Jake was still boxed in as tightly as ever. Now he rode northward across the land with her again, regretting the day he had ever laid eyes on Yvonne Blaine.

They rode on as the day began to fade and grow cooler. There was still no sign of Davenport and his men on their back trail, for which Jake was grateful. The land now spread out around them in a flat featureless expanse. At least there was no possibility of ambush. Still

Jake was not easy. He would have to kill Davenport, or make a successful escape from the territory to survive. In Bill Davenport's eyes Jake had stolen his woman and cheated him out of the freight-office money, and Jake did not think that the man would ever call a halt to his pursuit.

In a way Jake almost pitied the man. He had already lost the game, defeated in his ambitions by the dark-eyed haughty woman at his side. In a way, too, Jake almost pitied Yvonne: she had won, but still she had nothing. Maybe that would become clear to her someday, but Jake doubted it.

An eerie shrieking sound shattered the evening stillness, and it took Jake a moment to figure out what it had been. Then it sounded again and simultaneously he spotted a tiny, box-like structure ahead of them. Now, too, looking that way, he could see the late sun shimmering on the twin iron rails and a dark, beetle-sized creature racing toward them out of the west. Yvonne's face reflected excitement.

'We made it just in time! That's the east-bound train. We've beaten the odds.'

Her expression became smug again; perhaps she was thinking her own clever planning had turned the trick. Yvonne lifted her sorrel's pace and, as they approached the tiny water stop, the train which had appeared larger now, took on form. Jake frowned.

'I don't see any passenger cars — this is a freight run, that's all.'

'I don't care what it is,' Yvonne said, 'they'll find space for me.'

'You could wait for a passenger train,' Jake said, as they neared the water stop and slowed their ponies again.

'Wait? Is that what you'd do, Jake?'

'No, I guess not,' he conceded. 'I'd get out of here as soon as I could, any way I could.'

'And that is exactly what I intend to do,' Yvonne said.

The train was slowing for the station now, clanking and creaking as it positioned the locomotive beneath the huge spigot of the wooden water tank which loomed over the cracker-box station house. Yvonne swung down from the sorrel, negligently handed the reins to her servant, Jake, and started toward the building just as a white-haired man with a whiskered face and baggy trousers emerged to do his job. The station-master, Jake thought. He had a younger man, an Indian by the look of him, to do the actual work. Jake saw this one scrambling up the iron ladder to the water tower.

Yvonne was approaching the station master whose expression changed from curiosity to delight as she walked toward him as only Yvonne could, her long legs stretching out with each stride, deer-like, cat-like, provocative. Yvonne said something to him that Jake could not catch and the two went into the building as the water spout was lowered to mate with the locomotive's boiler.

Steam spewed skyward at first and

then the boiler cooled, drinking its fill. The train crew had stepped from the cab of the locomotive and from the red caboose to stand along the depot platform. A man Jake took to be the engineer mopped at his broad, perspiring face with a red handkerchief, watching as they waited for the boiler to fill, to be on their way eastward once again.

This was no regular station where they would have been given a meal. The water stop had no such amenities. It was simply a necessary delay along their route. Above them the Indian looked down from his perch, gauging the amount of water as it flowed into the locomotive. Experience must have taught him how much was needed, for he halted the flow of water before it could top off and spill from the boiler.

Jake wondered irrelevantly how the Indian had come to this lonely place, how his life could be out here in the desert. But then again, perhaps it was better than life on some scratch-earth reservation.

The door to the station house opened again and Yvonne emerged with the station master. She had a narrow blue paper in her hand. The station master rushed to catch up with the engineer before he could mount the locomotive's iron steps and the two men exchanged words briefly with the engineer shaking his head and then eventually pointing toward the rear of the train. The station master returned to tell Yvonne something, his toothless grin wide, his eyes bright. One more conquest for Yvonne, Jake awaited her return, watching the Indian scramble down the ladder, his work finished for the time being.

Yvonne walked along the platform to where Jake waited. 'It's all right,' she said, her face a little pink from excitement. 'I have a ticket, you see,' she said, showing him the blue ticket in her hand. 'I'm freight,' she laughed.

'Where are you supposed to ride?'

'Just along, there's supposed to be a

car with an open door. It has bales of hay to feed the livestock on board. He just said to find a loose bale and sit on it. The train stops again in two hours at a regular station, and then I can get a ticket on the next passenger train. By that time I'll be miles away from Bill Davenport — he'll have no chance of ever catching up with me. I'll be well on my way East,' she said, her eyes sparkling with triumph. The station master still stood in the doorway, watching her with admiration.

'You certainly charmed the old geezer,' Jake said as he led the horses along toward the open door of the freight ear containing fodder.

'Yes, I charmed him — with my purse,' Yvonne told him.

'I see,' Jake said. The bell rang from the front of the train. The engineer was impatient to be going. The train lurched forward a few feet even as Jake was helping Yvonne up into the freight car. It smelled of hay. Bales were stacked along the walls and loose wisps of the stuff littered the floor.

'It'll do,' Yvonne announced, glancing around. The train lurched forward again as Jake clambered aboard after her.

'You can't go along, Jake,' she said severely.

'No, I don't mean to,' Jake said. The train was now rolling slowly out of the station.

'Well then, you'd better get off — we're picking up speed.'

'Yes, we are. I just wondered, Yvonne, are you going to pay me for my work?'

'For your . . . I told you that you could take my horse.'

'Yes, you did,' Jake answered quietly, 'but I think I've already taken just about enough from you.'

'What do you mean?' she asked, clutching the green bag containing the stolen money nervously to her breast.

The train was accelerating rapidly now, the desert darkness blurring past them. Jake smiled faintly and then reached out. It wasn't much of an effort to tear the satchel from Yvonne's hands as she backed away from him fearfully.

'Let's talk this over, Jake.'

But with every second the train's speed was increasing, its iron wheels devouring the distances, and there was no more time for conversation. He moved to the open door, glanced out and tossed the bag as far ahead as possible and then leaped from the freight car. Landing on the sandy bank, he rolled over three or four times, came to his feet and stood watching the rear of the departing train. He thought that he could see Yvonne's angry face as she looked out of the car, but probably he did not at that distance. And when the train's whistle blew once again, he imagined that he could hear the sound of a furious harpy screaming out a curse against the night.

* * *

Under a cold moon in an empty night Jake rose, dusted himself off and began slogging through the sand back toward the station. Moving slowly, he searched the strip of earth beside the rails as he made his way, and eventually discovered the green satchel by moonlight. Picking it up, he started along heavily. He had not looked inside the satchel; frankly he did not care how much money was left inside, though he thought it must be almost all of the cash taken from the freight office.

The question was — now what was he going to do with it? He did not want it. He would have to give the matter some thought.

They had traveled farther down the line than he had believed, perhaps a mile, but finally he was able to make out the dim lights from the station, flickering in the night. He went on, his leg aching. He wanted badly to be back in the saddle again. He was still not fit enough for a long trudge on foot.

The shadow of the water tower's framework fell over him and he breathed with relief.

Four paces on the man with the shotgun emerged from the shadows to challenge Jake.

'What are you doing around here?' a soft voice demanded. As the man came nearer, Jake could see that it was the Indian who worked at the station.

'I just came back for my horse,' Jake said, trying to keep his manner casual. 'The lady and I had a parting of the ways.' The Indian might not have been able to recognize Jake from his perch on the water tower earlier, but he would have noticed the woman at that distance.

'Which one? The blue roan?' the man asked. 'The one with the bullet hole through its ear?'

'Yes,' Jake said, for he had already decided to continue on the blue roan since they were getting used to each other. The Indian's face was still dubious. Jake resorted to one of Yvonne's tricks: bribery.

'The lady isn't coming back,' Jake told the station hand. 'She gave me her horse. Now, I'd like to give it to you, if you want it.'

'The big sorrel?' the young Indian asked with a surge of excitement.

'That one — if you want it, of course,' Jake said as if he were indifferent to the idea.

'That is the finest horse I have ever seen,' the Indian said. Amazement showed on his face at the offer Jake had made and then the expression turned to doubt. People didn't just give such animals away. 'You are sincere?' he asked Jake.

'Completely sincere. If anyone asks you about it just tell them that a woman left on the train East and she gave you the horse.'

'It is not stolen, is it?' the man asked cautiously.

'No,' Jake said honestly, 'it is not stolen.'

By now the man was smiling, and his shotgun had been lowered. Jake said, 'Now if you can show me where my blue roan is, I'll be happy to ride away and leave you to your business.'

The problem was, Jake had no idea where he was going to ride once he was aboard the blue roan. The Indian was still fooling around with the sorrel, so Jake leaned out of the saddle to ask him, 'Any idea where I can find a town with a stable and a place for me to bed down out here?'

'Nothing for fifty miles, but if you're willing to make that long a ride tonight, there's a little place called Alma, just about due north from here.' The man pointed toward the north star. 'It's about a thousand feet up into the hills. I don't know why anybody ever settled there, but it's there.'

'You've never seen it?'

'Mister, it's the kind of place that they shoot Indians on sight. There's still a few like that left around. It seems the folks in Alma had a lot of trouble with the Utes not so many years ago, and any one with a red skin makes them nervous, no matter what tribe he's from.'

Jake nodded. 'It seems we all get branded whether we had anything to do with a problem or not.'

'Ain't that the truth. Well, good luck to you stranger, and thanks for the horse.'

Hitting the long, lonesome trail across the desert Jake just watched as the stars cast a silvery web across the sky and the lazy half-moon shrank and began its slow wheeling toward the west. There was nothing else to be seen across the empty land. No light, no beast, no man. Still he felt better than he had in the last few days since neither was there a plotting woman at his side.

The roan was holding up well, though it had many miles under it and was badly in need of food, water and rest. Gradually a rank of hills rose from the horizon as the night wore on. The hills where the town of Alma supposedly sat somewhere along their length. Man and horse were both weary by now. To search unknown hills for a hidden settlement seemed a huge task.

Jake had pulled up at an arroyo running east to west, tying to figure out a way to cross it. The arroyo was only a dark ribbon in the night, and the more dangerous for the darkness. He could not see a way down or up in this poor light. He couldn't risk taking a spill or having the roan break a leg. 'We just might not make it tonight,' Jake told the horse, which swiveled its damaged ear toward the sound of his voice.

The voice from out of the darkness was raw and unfamiliar. 'Ride along with me and I'll show you the crossing,' the unknown man said. Jake's hand had already dropped to the butt of his Colt, and now the stranger behind him said, 'Don't get antsy on me, son. I'm just one of those good Samaritans that the preachers talk about.'

Either that, or a man in perfect position to snatch the green satchel containing the stolen money from Jake's dead hands.

6

'The name's Webb Saunders,' the man who had appeared like a ghost from off the desert said, as he let his horse walk up beside where Jake Worthy sat the blue roan. The stranger did not offer his hand, nor did Jake.

Webb Saunders was a whiskered beanpole of a man, his skin as dry and leathery as the desert creatures Jake came across — armadillos, lizards, tortoises. The hot sun tortured all skin unmercifully, drying it, removing all of its moisture. Webb Saunders had a torn hat tugged down low despite the fact that it was dark and his eyes needed no shielding from sun glare. The shadow of the hat brim revealed a sharp, narrow, seemingly suspicious face, but Saunders' voice if whispery dry, seemed friendly enough. Jake decide to trust him for now. What else was there to do?

'If you just ride ahead about fifty yards or so, there's a broke-down bank we can follow to the bottom of the arroyo, and a little way along there's another ramp we can ride up to reach the far side. There's no trick to it, even at midnight, if you know the way.'

* * *

Jake was still wary as he followed the man along the rim of the wash. That would be a fine place to leave a dead man — he would never be found. Saunders had noticed the green satchel tied to Jake's saddle horn. Jake had seen his eyes flicker that way a few times. It was an unusual place for a rider to carry a part of his gear, though there could be many explanations for it.

Saunders led the way down into the dark maw of the night-shaded ravine, and Jake followed. The night was nearly completely black as they reached the sandy bottom where water ran, at most, twice a year with run-off from the nearby hills. The smell of sage was heavy in the air and the scent of unseen brackish pools of water. Twin sycamores like a pair of separated lovers faced each other across the sandy trail and blocked their way enough so that the men had to duck to cleat the low-hanging boughs.

'We cross over here,' Saunders announced, and by the scant light of the dully glowing night sky Jake could pick out the lighter sandy ramp leading up to the western edge of the ravine. He was not willing to extend endless gratitude to Webb Saunders, but Jake knew that that he would never have found the crossing on his own and would likely have had to spend the night on the hard ground beside the arroyo. Now he had at least some hope of finding a bed tonight and forage for his horse — Bill Davenport's horse, he reminded himself.

As they reached the flats again and started on, Jake asked Saunders, 'How far is it to Alma?'

106

'Alma? Is that where you're headed?'

'Is there any other place around here?'

'No,' Saunders said with a dry chuckle, 'there isn't.' He tipped his hat back and glanced toward the dark hills in front of them. 'It's ten, fifteen miles along, son, but unless you know the area, you're never going to ride that trail in the dark.'

'Is it rough?'

'Rough, snaky and dangerous,' Saunders replied. 'You've little chance of making Alma tonight. Whoever told you about that town?'

'Just a man I happened to run into. I don't know his name.'

'Well, he don't know the east Alma grade very well.'

'He said he'd never been there himself,' Jake told Saunders.

'Oh, well,' Webb Saunders muttered, 'I guess you might as well come home with me for the night'

'I don't need — '

'Of course you do. Look at the way your horse is carrying himself. He's tired, thirsty and beat down — you can't be in much better shape yourself. You can suit yourself, mister, but I do have hay and water, chow and an extra bed for you.'

Jake considered silently for awhile, looking around at the long barren land and the dark bulking hills which lay ahead. He didn't even have an idea of where he was riding.

'I'll take you up on your offer,' Jake said finally, 'if it's all right with you.'

'I made the offer, didn't I?' Saunders answered. 'We'll feed you and fill that horse up. You can always pay me later.'

Pay me later? What did Saunders mean by that, or was Jake simply getting jumpy, riding with all that stolen money? Jake had already decided what he was going to do with the green satchel and its contents. It could only bring him trouble. He meant to return it to Yvonne's father, Sam Blaine, at the freight office but he had no idea how to do that without dragging himself into more trouble. He was still one of the band of men who had robbed the place and kidnapped Yvonne. No amount of fast talking was going to convince people otherwise.

That lay in the future. For tonight he had no choice but to follow the old desert rat to his secluded hideout, wherever that might be. If he awoke alive in the morning, Jake thought, perhaps he could come up with an idea on how to continue on.

Webb Saunders now struck Jake as a companionable man, living a lonesome time on the vast, barren desert, happy for any company that might come his way. Jake's earlier forebodings about Saunders had been born of his own anxious suspicions, it seemed, and not because of anything the man of the desert had said or done. Saunders continued to talk as they rode on into the dark hills, Jake listening with only half of his attention, still wondering who might be on his back trail. Could anyone have followed him this far?

The desert night grew colder and

Saunders was hunched in his leather jacket. Jake had groped into the saddle-bags the roan was carrying and come up with a blanket which he put over his shoulders. The breath of the horses was a fog before their nostrils.

'How long have you been out here, Saunders?' Jake asked, his teeth chattering.

'Oh, I'm sort of the new man in the region. I haven't been around but about twenty years or so. Why, I've never seen but a single Indian since I came out here.'

'I've heard that the Utes once attacked Alma,' Jake said.

'I guess that's so — it's what everyone says, but I'm of the opinion that it was probably Apaches. 'Course I wasn't here, as I say. One day, early on, I was out hunting, since food was getting kind of scarce and I spotted a fine four-point mule deer buck, when out from behind this rock rises up a young Indian brave. He was armed with only a bow and arrows, but it was obvious that we were after the same deer, and that he meant to have it. I was pretty certain that he meant to kill me if he had to, to prevent me from taking the animal.

'Well, I began trying to solve things with a lot of sign language. Not really that because I knew none, but with a lot of pointing and gesturing. He didn't seem to take my meaning,' Saunders said, 'so I let my sights come around and I fired a shot through my old Spencer .50.'

'You killed him?' Jake asked in surprise. But Saunders laughed.

'No, son! Why would I do that? I dropped that mule deer buck and pulled out my knife, making a lot more gestures and finally the young brave nodded. We went down the hill and butchered the buck and split the meat fifty-fifty.'

'That was the last Indian I ever seen in these hills,' Saunders said almost wistfully. 'I stayed on. Nobody bothers a man out here. I got no clock and no calendar. I started building a little house with found lumber and all these years on I've got something built that suits me. It don't leak and it hasn't fallen down yet. I have to admit that it's not pretty, but, as I said, it suits me.'

'Don't you ever want more?' Jake asked, surveying the dark, empty hills. Saunders' voice was different when he answered, 'Son, I've had more. It didn't make me any happier.'

In relative silence then, they rode on. The moon was nearly dying in the west when Saunders gestured to Jake and they entered a narrow cleft in the rocky face of a low hill and followed a steep trail upward. Emerging, Jake found himself in front of a low, crudely-built house. Astonishingly, there was a light burning within. Saunders swung down heavily, loosened his horse's saddle cinch and led it to a narrow, home built wooden water trough. Jake followed suit.

Saunders was moving toward the doorway now and he waved a hand,

'Come on in, son.'

Warily, Jake walked to join him, carrying the green satchel tightly in his left hand. He wanted to be rid of the thing. It clouded his every thought with mistrust. Someone had taken the trouble to whitewash the face of the cabin and, as Jake drew nearer, he could see that someone had trained long thorny strands of bougainvillea to grow across the eaves of the building. A multitude of small purple-red flowers clung to the vine. Saunders gestured, removed his hat to reveal a mostly bald crown and entered the shack, Jake a step behind him.

A small shriek and drawn-out groan greeted them. 'Darnit, Dad, do you have to bring home everyone you run across? I never have enough food prepared for extra guests.' Jake looked toward the owner of the voice. A young woman, probably under twenty-five years of age, stood in the doorway of the house's open kitchen. She held a pot in one hand, a wooden spoon in the other. She was blonde, fairly tall, and nicely trimmed, Jake thought. She was also a little frustrated at the moment, not really angry with Saunders, but piqued.

'Sorry, Dosie,' Saunders muttered, fingering his hat like a schoolboy. 'What was I to do — the man was lost out on the desert.'

The girl, Dosie, sighed heavily. 'I know, Dad,' she said, wiping away a stray tendril of hair which had fallen across her smooth forehead with the back of her hand. 'We'll make do. We always do.'

Saunders chuckled as the girl went back into the kitchen. 'My daughter,' he told Jake. 'She never really gets mad at me. If she does it doesn't last long.'

'Maybe I should camp outside,' Jake suggested.

'No, don't be silly. I think mostly Dosie's afraid that I'll pick up the wrong man some day and get myself hurt. And I may, come to think of it,' he added thoughtfully. He tossed his hat toward a roughly made, carelessly covered sofa and put his hand on Jake's shoulder. 'The girl says she doesn't like me bringing in strangers — often they're wounded or deprived men. But she's the same. We saw an old dog that had been hit by a freight wagon down in Alma town. Anyone could see the poor animal didn't have a chance of making it, but Dosie made me bring it all the way back here with us. She nursed the thing day after day. It died, of course; it was all torn up inside. She buried it out back herself while I was gone. We never spoke of it again.'

Jake's nerves were still no good. The money in the green satchel caused that. For one instant he wondered if it had been a dog that Saunders was talking about. Crazy thoughts!

'Come to the table, men!' Dosie called cheerfully. Apparently her irritation had only been a momentary thing like any woman might feel if her man brought unexpected company home for supper.

Around a small, rough table they settled into a meal of ham, yams and mustard greens. Dosie apologized for the meal, but it suited Jake fine.

Later, sitting in front of the native-stone fireplace while Saunders smoked his pipe and the wavering light cast by the low fire danced across the room, painting primitively comforting patterns, Jake asked, 'Where do you get yams from — way out here?'

'That's all Dosie's doing. She has a little box garden out back. Every time we go to town she buys one of those little packets of vegetable seeds and tends those that can stand the desert heat.'

'She does a little bit of everything, doesn't she?' Jake commented. In the kitchen he could still see the girl's slender back as she scrubbed up the supper dishes. He thought he could hear her whistling under her breath. 'I mean the vegetables, cooking and cleaning. I saw the whitewash on the front of the house, the flowers planted there.'

'She's a treasure, my Dosie,' Saunders said, blowing out a wreath of blue tobacco smoke, watching it as it drifted toward the low ceiling.

'She must get tired of living out here, sometimes.'

'She must, but Dosie doesn't complain.'

Jake was silent for a minute, then asked, 'What happened to her mother?'

Saunders shrugged. 'She and I just didn't see eye to eye after awhile,' Saunders said. 'That was long ago, before I even came out here.' Jake glanced toward Saunders, unsure if the man was through speaking. Saunders' eyes were intent on the flickering fire. He held his pipe in one hand and sat leaning forward as if there were secrets of some sort hidden among the twisting flames in the fireplace. Jake saw Saunders' lips twist and form a word which he spat out silently against the flames. It was one word only; Jake could read it on his lips: *tramp*.

Jake decided that their conversation

was done for the night. Stretching, he asked Saunders, 'Where do I bunk?'

'Dosie will show you,' he said wearily. In fact Saunders looked suddenly tired. He did not look up as Jake rose. The man seemed to have aged ten years in the past few minutes. Jake determined not to ask any more questions concerning Dosie's mother. Some things are hard to forgive; others, it seems, are never forgiven.

'I should take care of my horse first,' Jake said, as he stood behind Saunders who had not moved an inch. Saunders waved a hand.

'I'll see to that,' the old man said. 'Get yourself some rest.' Jake murmured his thanks and walked to the kitchen where Dosie was just finishing up, drying her hands on a small towel. 'Your father said you would show me where I can sleep,' Jake said.

'Certainly,' Dosie said without expression, placing the towel aside.

Still wearing her apron Dosie led the way across the cramped house along a narrow corridor. It was dark along the way; the fireplace was the only light offered in the cabin. Unerringly Dosie found a small room and opened the door. It wasn't as large as your average closet. Dosie stepped aside and let Jake squeeze in past her. The room was furnished with a bed. Nothing more.

'Sorry we can't do better,' Dosie — or rather Dosie's silhouette — said.

'It's better than anything else I had offered tonight, and better than other places I have slept,' he added, thinking about the prison cell he and Eric Grove had once shared. His eyes were slowly adjusting to the darkness and now he made a point of studying the door to the tiny room, assuring himself that there was no lock on it. He was traveling wary, deep in suspicion, nearly fearful — if he didn't get rid of that stolen money soon, they'd find him running naked on the desert, baying at the moon.

Jake slept soundly, or at least peacefully. His leg had nearly quit acting up on him. The darkness of the tiny room was almost complete as he pried his eyes open, though his inner clock told him that it must be nearly dawn. He thought that if he searched around blindly he could probably find a lantern or at least a candle, but instead of wasting the time he groped his way to the door and swung it wide. The hallway was bathed in a pale-gray light and he could smell a fresh fire being started in the hearth, meant to remove the night chill from the cabin. Jake had not bothered to remove his boots the night before. He found his hat on the floor where he had left it and went out.

From somewhere a dull orange light seeped into the cabin's interior. There was no one in the living room, no one in the kitchen, but there by the early light cast through the narrow window, he could see a pot boiling on the stove, its spout beginning to steam. Someone, Dosie probably, was making coffee. The aroma was intense and pleasurable in the small room. Jake seated himself at the narrow, rickety table to wait.

Idly, Jake looked around the room, small but neatly arranged, and then impatiently rose to look out the rear window. He saw Dosie standing next to a clothes-line, pinning up her laundry. She wore a checked blue dress this morning, and it suited her well. Her blonde hair was worn stacked on top of her head in a casual-appearing but attractive style.

Watching her work, her lips pursed in concentration, smelling the coffee boiling on the stove brought a tiny feeling of both loneliness and delight to Jake. He could imagine himself in his own house, watching Becky Holland go about her chores, sipping coffee that she had boiled for him.

The hell with it he thought, shaking his head — that is what you get when you go away or allow yourself to be taken away. You miss out on all of life's small pleasures. He had missed out on so much.

Not for long, he swore to himself. He

would return the stolen money to Samuel Blaine and then be on his way back to Rio Lobo, searching for that elusive normal life that others had. He, Jake knew, would appreciate it now far more than your ordinary man. And as far as trouble went, he was done with it in any shape or form.

The front door swung open and Jake heard Webb Saunders call out, 'Dosie! Come here and look who I've found!'

Curious, Jake walked into the living room to see Saunders and the man with him.

It was the bug-eyed Sparky Finnet, and the bloated little outlaw's eyes flickered vengefully and he bared his yellow teeth as his hand dropped to his holstered pistol.

7

Sparky Finnet was pretty fast, but he was also too enraged to have a steady hand and when he fired, his bullet sung off of something in the kitchen and whined into the wall. Jake Worthy's gun hand was calmer, his aim surer, and the A4 slug from his Colt caught Finnet with a solid, deadly thud.

Sparky had been turned slightly to his right when he had fired, jerking around at the sight of Jake Worthy. Jake's bullet had taken him low on the right side, beneath the last ribs and near the liver, and exited the back of the bad man's body through his spine. Sparky Finnet fell with his pistol still in hand, but there was no way he was going to rise from the rough cabin floor to fire again. The little toad lay on his back, legs dancing an involuntary jig, his face washed to sheet-white, his mouth twisted as he tried to swallow his pain.

Jake crossed the room, holstering his Colt and kicked Finnet's pistol from his limp, twitching fingers. Dosie, summoned by her father's earlier call, spurred on by the sudden explosion of gunfire, burst in through the front door, anxious eyes surveying the scene. She rushed toward Saunders, briefly clinging to him. Her eyes fixed on Jake Worthy as he crossed the room and kicked Finnet's gun aside.

'What's going on here?' Dosie demanded. She looked toward the body on the floor. 'Isn't that — '

'Sparky Finnet,' Webb Saunders said, in a low, pained voice. 'He always stopped by when he was traveling east,' he explained to no one.

Dosie had stepped to Finnet's body and crouched down over it. 'He's alive!' she said in astonishment. Truthfully Finnet did not look like a man who should be alive, as much damage as Jake's bullet had done, but she could feel a pulse in his throat. 'Help me get him up on to the couch.'

Jake simply stepped away as Saunders came to help lift Finnet's still form on to the couch, his body dripping blood on to the floor in small, urgent drops. The man hadn't long to live; that seemed certain. Dosie fixed a heated gaze on Jake who had not moved a step to help them. 'What are you doing?' she demanded harshly. Jake noticed that her nose crinkled up when she was very angry. It didn't seem like the time to mention it. Instead he answered coldly, 'I'm just trying to decide whether to spit on him or just finish him off with another bullet.'

'Don't you dare think of it!' Dosie commanded.

'Spitting?' Jake asked innocently.

'Shooting him again! It's likely you've already killed him, though I can't guess why, and I don't suppose you'd care to tell us.'

'The man took a shot at me at point-blank range. I take offense at things like that.'

'Father?' Dosie asked, looking up at Saunders whose mouth was drawn down heavily in sorrow.

'Finnet did shoot first — though I don't know why either. I don't suppose Jake is going to tell us that.' There was no reply from Jake Worthy. He hadn't the time to tell the whole story, and it would likely only make him seem worse.

'We've got to get him into the spare bedroom.' She looked at Jake. His room, she meant. 'I can cut his shirt off and at least clean and bind the wound.'

Jake had never seen a liver or a fractured spine that could be bound, but he said nothing. He turned and started away, out the back door of the cabin, into the clean, heated day. He had wanted to tell Dosie that trying to treat what was left of Sparky Finnet was as doomed to failure as her attempt to rescue the dog that had been run over by a freight wagon. But what would have been the point in saying that to her?

Outside, Jake moved around aimlessly for awhile. He found the dog's grave near the bluff which thrust up behind the house. Dosie had placed a circle of whitewashed stones around it. At least the dog had died being loved and cared for. Jake wondered who would take any such trouble with his grave. He tried to drive away the gloomy thought as he walked toward the lean-to stable, passing Dosie's wooden box garden which held tiny rows of heat-parched vegetables that Jake could not identify by their tops.

The blue roan stood next to a dark bay gelding Jake took for Finnet's mount in the scant shade of the lean-to. The horse had enough water and hay, and so Jake just stroked the animal's sleek neck. He was actually growing fond of the horse. Too bad he would have to be getting rid of it soon. There were too many sharp-eyed citizens in Belmont who might have seen the somewhat distinctive horse either standing in front of the freight office, or being ridden away from the scene of the robbery.

Jake gave the blue roan a final affectionate slap on the shoulder and went out again into the brilliant glare of day, but not before sizing up the place enough to notice a corner where he could sleep that night. Morning would be soon enough to head out — Jake did not wish to ride through the heat of the day in this country. Alma, he had decided, by tomorrow, then another day on to Belmont. He was determined to return the money, and now twisted and turned mentally trying to come up with a way to do it without being dragged into the robbery's aftermath.

Then — if he could effect the plan — it was a straight line and what would be a rapidly ridden one back to Rio Lobo where he had again left Becky Holland waiting. How long had it been this time? Six months and however many days he had been tangled up in the latest complications. Small complications: only robbery, horse-stealing, kidnapping, maybe even murder. Could he really manage to return the cash to the freight office and elude the law on those charges?

There was reason to doubt it, and after all of the promises he had made to Becky Holland, written to her from prison, she would never accept these fresh episodes of his life, nor totally believe in his innocence again if he told her of them.

Walking again past the back yard of the house he came to a ledge where he could look out at the dark tangle of hills and arroyos which hid the long trail out. The distance must be too long, but still he had vaguely hoped to catch a glimpse of the tiny settlement of Alma — some wisp of smoke, sunlight striking a glass window, a patch of color, but there was nothing, just nothing. The broken hills led into the obscure distance, reminding Jake of his unfortunate life.

'Alma is beyond that knob. You can just barely see the trail circling it.'

Dosie Saunders stood just behind and beside Jake, a pointing finger raised toward the horizon. Her tone was neutral; the lingering anger seemed to have abated. Jake turned, tried a smile which was not returned and asked, 'Why are you trying to help me?'

Her eyes shifted away. She said, 'You can't believe I want you staying around here a minute longer than necessary.'

'No,' Jake muttered, looking into the distance again, 'I guess you wouldn't.' He wanted to ask her a few questions, but decided that now was not the time. As he watched, she went to her sad little garden and crouched down to weed it.

Not another word passed between them. Feeling forlorn, Jake returned to the stable and curried the blue roan until its coat shone. Then he spent some time working on his saddle — Bill Davenport's saddle. The stirrups had been just a little short since he had first stepped aboard the horse. There had been little time for adjusting them before. He positioned the hay in the corner of the lean-to and placed a blanket over it. That was to be his bed for the night. It did not matter; he had slept in worse places.

Finally, having run out of ways to kill time, Jake went out into the glow of the lowering sun. He reckoned that there was only another hour or so of light. When night fell he would go to the house, eat if they would feed him, and return to the lean-to to roll up in his blanket. Tomorrow he would rise with the dawn and be on his way — toward Alma, if he could find the small settlement among the tangle of hills and canyons.

He would at least be away from Webb Saunders' house, which would please Dosie. For a time then Jake sat on a rounded gray boulder, watching the sky color and begin to darken, splitting wisps of hay with his thumbnails. When he judged the time to be right, he made his way to the back door, smelling something appetizing on the stove.

Saunders met him as he entered the house.

'Wondered where you'd gotten to,' the old man said.

'Just trying to stay out of the way,' Jake replied.

Saunders' eyes grew softer, sadder. 'No need to feel that way, son. I don't know what caused it, but it seems there was bad blood between you and Sparky Finnet, and I did see the man draw first on you . . . I should never have brought him around here.'

'You couldn't have known. It's not your fault,' Jake told him.

'No, I couldn't. Still a man feels a little funny when he's caused something like this to happen . . . come on, let's get to the table while the food's hot.'

They walked to the table, Saunders' arm across Jake's shoulders. Already seated, Dosie lifted poisonous eyes to Jake and bent her gaze to her bowl. Jake seated himself uncomfortably and took a bowl of white beans and ham, a wedge of cornbread that Saunders

132

offered him. He did not look up at the silent Dosie throughout the meal. Saunders tried to start a general discussion about mostly unimportant things, but eventually gave it up. Jake was angry enough that he offered the cook no praise for her meal — something his late father would have frowned upon. 'A woman slaves away over that stove just to please you, the least you can do is let her know you appreciate it,' he had told Jake on more than one occasion. It was simple manners, but Jake was out of simple manners just then. He folded his napkin and rose.

'I'd better be turning in. I mean to hit the trail early in the morning.'

Saunders only nodded; Dosie didn't even look up.

Jake went out into the darkness, watching as a few stars began to twinkle across the sky. The land had not yet begun to cool. It would have been a nice evening to be out sitting on a porch, drinking coffee and talking, but it was not the night for it. There was no one around who would appreciate his company just now.

Jake made his way to the lean-to and settled down on the hasty bed he had made, listening to the occasional noises the horses made as they shifted their feet or blew through their nostrils. Jake closed his eyes and waited for sleep, which did not come easily.

* * *

There was an utter stillness in the nearly-complete darkness of the room where Sparky Finnet lay. The girl had come to try to get him to eat something, but Finnet had no appetite. The pain he felt was exquisite, terrible. In the darkness he wondered if he were already dead, but figured he was not as the pain surged again. He had not yet breathed his last, which meant there was still a chance. A chance to take Jake Worthy along with him into the fiery depths of hell. He had wanted to kill Jake Worthy ever since they had come across him in the White Mountains, but Bill Davenport would have his way and held him back.

It could not be called sleeping, but as the night went on Sparky Finnet passed out from lingering shock and loss of blood, entering an almost painless realm of semi-consciousness. When he awoke it was to a flare of pain and a rush of furious hatred. He cradled the only hope for his future in his right hand. His cold blue revolver. With it, he thought, he could force them to deliver him to a real doctor. He did not care if he ever walked again; he just wanted to survive.

Long enough to end Jake Worthy's life.

The night passed slowly — intervals of angry pain and hatred and then a slow slide into unconsciousness.

Finnet was bathed in perspiration when he awoke again just before daylight. He did not know the time, could not guess it in his dark room, but he thought he had heard a few morning birds beyond the flimsy walls of the cabin, chirping to greet the morning sun. Their sound was damnable; he despised their cheeriness. Then he heard the slow approach of footsteps along the hall.

Finnet knew who it was — Jake Worthy come to finish him off. And to reclaim the stolen money. As battered as he was, still he had seen and recognized the green canvas bag half-concealed beneath the bed. It was the same one Yvonne Blaine had been holding when she faced him in the freight office. Now Worthy had it, somehow gotten it from Yvonne.

Sweat still trickled into Sparky Finnet's eyes as he lay in bed, listening. It took a mighty effort for him just to ear back the hammer of the big Colt revolver, but he had done it and now he lay waiting for the traitor to the gang to enter the room and try to finish Sparky off. Finnet smiled; Worthy would discover that Sparky Finnet did not die so easily.

The door opened just a crack on oiled hinges, swinging inward. Then the man filled the doorway and entered the room, wanting his revenge and his loot.

Sparky Finnet pulled the trigger and the Colt .44 thundered in the darkness of the tiny room. The intruder took the bullet full in the chest, and Sparky's head dropped back on to his damp pillow. He knew now that he was not going to make it, but it did not matter any more. Jake Worthy was on his way to hell with him.

The gun dropped from Sparky Finnet's fingers and clattered to the wooden floor of the cabin.

★   ★   ★

Jake Worthy's head came up and he scrambled from his makeshift bed in the lean-to as the startled horses watched him with apprehensive eyes.

Jake made his way to the front of the lean-to where gray morning light could be seen beyond the rising hills.

Who . . . ? He saw no horses that might have been ridden by visiting riders. There was no one around the outside of the cabin. The shot, then, had come from within. Grimly he made his way toward the cabin's back door, his hand on the butt of his holstered pistol. He paused as a shrill cry, an anguished, nerve-chilling scream like one from the throat of a wounded banshee sounded.

Jake hesitated at the rear door, then burst through, drawing his Colt. He started first toward the living room, but it was empty. He then strode carefully along the hallway, seeing a figure slumped against the floor, holding another inert form. He recognized Dosie even in the poor light.

'What's happened?' he asked the sobbing woman.

'Oh, dear God, it's my father. He's dead! Finnet shot him.'

Jake's mouth tightened as he stepped past them, kicked the door to the room open and entered moving in a crouch. By the dim light he saw Finnet, slack in his bed, the pistol on the floor beside him. Finnet's eyes were open, but the man was finally dead.

'What happened?' Jake asked the trembling girl.

'Father must have come to check up on Sparky, maybe to ask if he thought he could eat anything this morning . . . and Finnet killed him.'

'But why?'

'Because Sparky thought it was you, coming back to give him the second bullet you promised him!' Her voice was strangled by fury. Dosie took one step toward Jake, her hands fisted. 'It's your fault this happened,' she screamed. 'You had the man terrorized!'

Jake nodded, holstering his pistol. The glare in his eyes was visible in the gray light of dawn, the anger behind them. He asked softly, 'How did Finnet get his gun back, Dosie?'

She froze, her mouth falling open just a bit. She turned her head away. 'I gave it to him,' she stuttered. 'He was so afraid of you! He asked me to give it to him, and I . . . ' She was choking on her sobs now. Jake's face was set grimly as he pushed his way past her and walked toward the back door.

It was not his house, his job or his duty, but Jake paused enough to start some coffee boiling in the kitchen on his way out. He would need some kind of stimulant to get him through this morning.

Outside, he glanced at the tightening skies, saw a flock of doves winging their way somewhere across the desert, and returned to the lean-to to saddle the blue roan. There was nothing whatever to be gained by remaining here any longer.

Leading the roan outside, he saw Dosie Saunders dragging the dead Sparky Finnet out of the back door. Her face was intent, yet somehow without expression. She puffed as she towed the corpse across the hard-packed earth of the yard to where Webb Saunders already lay, his arms crossed over his chest.

Dosie glanced up as Jake appeared, leading the blue roan. A strand of hair had fallen over her eyes. She watched Jake's slow approach silently.

'I could use some help,' she said in a small voice. Jake shook his head as if with weariness.

'You'll have to clean up your own mess — you're the one who got your father killed.'

'It only happened because of you,' Dosie responded through her sniffles.

'Oh, I see. Then if everything had worked out to your satisfaction, I would be lying there instead of your father. That would have made you much happier. Sorry, lady, I'm climbing into the saddle and leaving.'

'You can't . . . ' Dosie began. Her lower lip was trembling.

'Sure I can,' Jake answered, trying to make his tone ironically amiable. 'I told you — clean up your own mess.'

'You, too,' she spat back. 'Don't forget your money when you leave. Sparky told me all about it last night

— that's why I let him have his gun back.'

'Sparky didn't know the truth about what actually happened, and if he had, he would have lied to you anyway.'

'You're right, you'd better get going,' Dosie said, a little more firmly now. 'It's for the best.'

Jake tramped into the house. He poured himself a cup of the strong coffee and set it aside to cool while he went to recover the green satchel containing the freight office's money. The room was as cold as a battlefield after the guns have passed. The bed still was in tangled disarray, stained heavily by Finnet's blood. Jake slid the green bag out from under the bed and opened the satchel to assure himself that its contents had not been disturbed. Then he returned to the kitchen and sipped at his cup of coffee.

Beyond the window he could hear Dosie pecking at the hard earth with her tools; it was a futile sort of sound. Jake glanced out. Resigned to her job, she worked away. It was almost fruitless; the hard-packed, dry earth barely showed signs of her assault. With her skirt now tucked up in her waistband, blonde hair dripping across her face, she gave Jake to wonder if this was all that a woman ever stood to gain out on this harsh desert, or anywhere at all throughout all time.

Placing his coffee cup down, he walked out into the dull light of day. There was a pick leaning against the wall of the cabin, and he picked it up as he walked toward the gravesite.

8

It was already desert-hot when they had finished scratching graves in the poor soil for the two dead men and rolled them into their final resting places. Dosie's mood had changed again, but her face was somber when she returned with coffee for Jake who sat now in the ribbon of shade cast by the rising bluff behind the house, the hot wind slowly drying the perspiration from his body.

He thanked Dosie for the cup and she seated herself cross-legged beside him, looking into the distances. He could not read the expression in her eyes.

'Thanks for helping me,' she said, without looking at him. 'I don't know how long it would have taken me alone.'

'Burying your father was no more than an unhappy privilege,' Jake replied. 'He treated me fine. As for Finnet — well, we even bury dogs around here, don't we?'

'Is that what he was — a dog?'

'No. Just some sort of creature masquerading as a man.'

'I never saw much difference between the two,' Dosie said, shifting her gaze so that her eyes met Jake's.

'I don't get you,' he replied. Jake stood, pulled his shirt away from his chest and let the air circulate there. 'What do you mean?'

'What does a dog do?' Dosie asked, now concentrating on her thought. 'They snarl and fight with each other at the drop of a hat. Roll in the dirt and don't know enough to clean themselves up. They wolf their food — they'll eat in three bites. If you make the mistake of showing them any attention, patting their head, for example, they immediately roll over and offer you their belly to rub.

'Really, Jake, is that much different from the way men behave?'

'I guess not.'

'How do you live that way? How do men do it?' she asked with a hint of disgust.

'You just get used to it, I guess. The only thing I can't do is scratch behind my ear with my hind leg.' He grinned and she laughed, just faintly.

'And that's all that separates you from the dogs?'

'Maybe, but I'll say this for a dog — he's always loyal, so loyal that he would lay down his life for you.'

'Is that how you see yourself?' Dosie wanted to know.

Changing the topic abruptly, Jake asked her, 'What are you going to do now, Dosie? Surely you don't plan on staying on out here?' He surveyed the barren land around them. The heat was still almost unbearable, even in the shade.

'No,' she said quietly. 'I only stayed on for Dad — he loved it out here in the wilderness. I've got a friend in Alma named Marie. She once told me she'd find me a job there in a little restaurant she owns if I ever decided that I wanted to come down out of the hills.'

'And do you?'

'I think I have to, and that's an even better reason. To try living alone out here without . . . even a dog, it just wouldn't work; I can see that now.'

Jake nodded thoughtfully, finishing his coffee.

'There's no point in lingering,' Dosie said. 'I'm leaving as soon as I can — I'll ride with you when you go.'

The reply surprised Jake, but he could think of no reason that they should not ride together — she knew the way and he carried the guns. Not that he feared being waylaid, but Sparky Finnet had inadvertently run into him. What about Bill Davenport and Eric Grove? Had they given it up by now, perhaps figuring that Yvonne had gone East with the money, or had they also some inkling that Jake Worthy would have taken it, given the opportunity? It was hard to tell. They might come looking, he knew. Since there was no way they could ever hope to catch up with Yvonne, riding the rails East. The West was broad, but only sparsely settled. There were few towns in this part of the country, and they would focus their search on these.

For even thousands of stolen dollars could not coerce a man to ride the desert country forever; it could not sustain him. He would have to light somewhere sooner or later. In some remote, out of the way place . . . like Alma.

While Dosie returned to her daily chores — watering her garden and then cleaning the tumbledown shack which likely would never be used or seen again, Jake walked back to the lean-to, feeling a little soreness in his shoulders. He was not used to pick and shovel work. The blue roan was still saddled, and it looked at Jake in confusion. Jake swung into leather and settled the horse, saying, 'All right then, we'll go out at least long enough for you to stretch out your muscles.'

It was an hour before sunset when Jake returned from touring the raw surrounding countryside, and it was still far from cool. Stabling the roan again, Jake walked to the back door of the house, but as his hand reached for the knob, he became aware of a small, mewling sound within. It was Dosie, finally letting out her grief in a series of muffled sobs. Jake turned away from the door and strode back to the lean-to where he sat on his straw bed, watching the silent night go purple and then slowly fade to black.

*   *   *

In the murky pre-dawn light Jake Worthy saddled the blue roan once again and threw a saddle over the back of Webb Saunders' patient horse. Who knew, Dosie might have changed her mind about leaving overnight, but he did not intend to wait for her decision. He was leaving for Alma this morning.

149

He led the two saddled animals and Sparky Finnet's bay to the back of the house. Surprisingly the back door to the house was already open. Coffee was on to boil.

Wearing trail clothes — a white, long-sleeved blouse, black jeans and a wide-brimmed, fawn-colored hat, Dosie appeared from the interior of the house, carrying a bedroll.

'Drink a cup of coffee,' she instructed him. 'I'm nearly ready.'

Jake nodded, wondering what 'nearly ready' meant to the woman. The roll she carried out and tied on behind the saddle of her father's horse contained nothing he could see but a blanket, a red-and-black checked shirt and a spare pair of blue jeans. Surely there was more. In his experience most women didn't feel comfortable moving unless they could take half of the contents of their house along. But that was all Dosie had. She did not return to her room, but busied herself filling canteens from the water barrel outside.

Then she immediately swung into leather, hands crossed on the pommel. 'Ready?' she called, and Jake gulped down the rest of his coffee, placed the cup aside and walked out into the gray light of morning, swinging into the blue roan's saddle.

'Who's the tagalong?' Dosie asked, as they started out of the yard. She nodded her head toward the unsaddled bay horse.

'It was Finnet's horse. There's no way it would make it out here on its own, and there's no reason it should pay for its owner's mistakes.'

Dosie smiled as if at some secret joke, but she said nothing as they guided their mounts down through the notch toward the trail below. 'That's that,' Dosie said in a near-whisper, as they reached the road. There was relief and nostalgia both in her tone. No matter how tough life had been out here, there's always something difficult about leaving a place where you have sheltered for years, enjoyed small pleasures and suffered pain and unhappiness. Most people can become creatures of habit easily if only because it is somehow reassuring to wake in a place you know, know what the day is likely to bring.

To Jake Worthy that was a feeling with which he was unfamiliar.

They followed the trail downward and came upon what looked to be a seldom-used path stretching westward. Brush grew up on either side of the trail, nearly hiding it, but Dosie had lived here for many years, and knew her way. The sun had risen beyond the bluffs and the long shadows of horses and riders stretched out before them. There was total silence except for the steady clomping of the horses' hoofs and now and then the call of a meadowlark as it took to wing.

'Do you want to tell me?' Dosie asked, as they reached a more traveled road that skirted the dark knoll Jake had seen from the Saunders cabin. Her voice was soft, interested, a pleasant distraction from the long ride through brush country and the silence of the cool morning. Jake twisted his head toward her.

'Tell me what really happened,' she said. 'You told me that Sparky Finnet didn't know the truth of things. You must. Why don't you tell me all about it? We still have a long ride ahead of us.'

'Are you sure you're really interested?' he asked, his voice dropping. Her attitude up to now had offended his sense of dignity. Petty, he knew, but he hadn't liked the woman doubting him.

'Of course I am,' Dosie said. Jake nodded, removed his hat and wiped his brow with his cuff.

'All right, then — here's how it happened.'

Gathering his concentration, he took in a deep breath and began telling Dosie his story as they wove their way down a snaking trail on the shadow side of a hill. There was no short way to tell it and so he began with the shooting of the gambler, Ned Quirk and his imprisonment for it and went straight through his long story. As Dosie had said, it was a long trail and he had plenty of time to tell his tale.

He told her of the day he had stepped out of prison and continued on to the shooting of Sparky Finnet at the Saunders' cabin, leaving nothing out.

It was long in the telling, but Dosie did not interrupt. She rode slightly ahead of him, her eyes on the trail. They were in sunlight once again, having reached flat ground beyond the hills when she said finally, 'I believe you. No one has enough imagination to invent that story. I'm only sorry I didn't know earlier. I had no idea why you shot Sparky Finnet. He was hardly great company, but he had been by our place a few times over the years and never caused any trouble. You, I had just met.'

Jake just nodded. Truthfully he was growing tired of discussing his own ragged life. Dosie had not. 'So you plan to return the freight office money when you can figure out how.'

'If I can figure out a way, yes.'

'Surely there are a number of methods you could use — you could find some middleman to deliver the loot, for example.'

'Yes . . . if I knew anyone I could trust, and I don't even know a soul in Belmont. If someone was given the money and failed to hand it over to Samuel Blaine, I'd be obligated to go after him and start the business up all over again.'

'There's a way,' Dosie said confidently. 'You'll figure it out.' She actually smiled at him; it had been a long time since he had seen her smile. Jake only nodded again. Dosie went on, 'Then you would start on your way to Rio Lobo again, wouldn't you? To meet this Becky Holland who's been waiting all this time for you?'

'That's always been the plan,' Jake said. 'Only now — darn it, Dosie — I wonder if the woman will still be there to welcome me back. I've let her down again. All I had to do was step on to a stagecoach . . . ' He fell off into silent brooding.

'You'd be surprised at a woman's capacity for waiting for the man she loves,' Dosie said.

'Maybe, but I've also seen many who will wave them goodbye and then sashay up to the next waiting male.'

'Has that happened to you, Jake?' Dosie asked, frowning.

'No, but I sure have seen it happen.'

'Either way, you'll find out. I doubt that Becky has waited this long only to toss you aside'

'She'd have good cause,' Jake grumbled.

Dosie thought for a moment, than said, 'Maybe the trouble is that you're lumping all of us together. Is Becky Holland anything like this Yvonne Blaine, for example?'

'No woman is like Yvonne,' Jake said with half a laugh. 'I pity the next man who tangles with her.'

'Well, so you see . . . ' Dosie said.

'Why *Dosie?*' Jake asked, tired again of discussing his own problems which still seemed unsolvable. 'I mean . . . it's an odd name, isn't it?'

Dosie laughed lightly. 'Not so unusual as you might think, I'd wager. I was christened Dorothy, but that's a mouthful for a baby. I called myself Dosie and pretty soon everyone else was calling me that, too. Besides,' she said, 'I don't really care for the name Dorothy anyway.'

Jake nodded his understanding. Ahead of them he saw the sudden flicker of sunlight striking something reflective and, as they crested a low, brush-covered knoll he could see the sun shining on panes of glass.

'Alma,' Dosie said wearily. They had been in the saddle for a long time, and she was relieved. Yet Jake could see concern in her eyes. He thought he understood that. She had taken her first concrete step into a new life. The old way was dead, and she could not know what the new one held.

'What if Marie has forgotten her

157

promise?' Dosie said almost to herself. 'What if she has given it up and no longer even lives here anymore?'

'We'll find out,' Jake said as calmly as he could. He smiled at Dosie. 'Let's hold up here for a minute — I've got to cut Finnet's horse free. It's very likely stolen, probably out of Belmont. We don't need anyone asking about it.'

It was bad enough that he was still riding Bill Davenport's blue roan. They needed no further complications. Setting the dark bay free, he slapped it on the rump. It might take a while, but it would find its way to Alma sooner or later to become someone else's problem.

They entered the town of Alma cautiously as the late sun began to shadow the rough community, hiding storefronts in shadow. The town was mostly silent, there being no reason for such an isolated settlement to be in any sort of uproar. Alma was just a place where people came to get battered by the sun, work themselves to the bone, and die. He wondered, as he often did, how the early settlers had sought out and built these small settlements which seemed to exist only because they existed.

'Where's Marie live?' Jake asked as they neared the town. Now they could see men and women — dark figures in this light — moving along the streets.

'Just west of here. I know the way, but I don't know if she'll be at home or at work.'

'Let's find out,' Jake suggested. He had no wish to enter any town, no matter how small, just then. Every man seemed a threat, every shadow to be holding trouble. Dosie led off, skirting the town. Within fifteen minutes they had come upon a group of four little white cottages, all obviously built according to the same plan standing near a healthy grove of mature cotton-wood trees. Dusk was settling prettily. The western skies were flushed pink, a settling deep purple making incursions.

'Which one is it?' Jake asked,

studying the four cabins.

'The one on the right. Here,' she said with certainty. 'Though I've only been here once before, I recognize it.'

'All right,' Jake said, as they halted before the cottage where a lantern glimmered low in the window. 'You'd better go up and see what sort of welcome you get.' At Dosie's curious look he asked, 'How long ago was it that she offered you that invitation?'

'Maybe a year,' Dosie replied. 'Why?'

'Maybe the offer was only made off the top of her head. Things change. Maybe Marie has a husband and a baby by now.'

'You're encouraging,' Dosie said, swinging down from her horse.

'I'm just saying that times change, people change. Get on up there now, Dosie. Find out what she's thinking.'

Jake was certainly not going with her. He had not been invited and was uninvolved in the women's business. It did feel good to get down from the saddle and stretch his legs while their two horses foraged for tidbits among the dry grass of the yard. The sky went dark and the moon began to rise — huge and yellow above the eastern mountains, it glazed the yard, trees and surrounding desert prettily.

Dosie returned, smiling broadly. Behind her the door remained ajar. Jake caught a quick glimpse inside of a young, small woman with dark hair. 'How did it go?' Jake asked, although her expression told him.

'Great! Marie has an extra room — it's decorated prettily, Jake. You should see it! She told me she really has been hoping to find another girl to help her at the restaurant, but there aren't that many around.'

'That restaurant work can be pretty hard,' Jake said, leaning across his saddle to watch as Dosie recovered her few belongings.

'I'm hardly a stranger to hard work,' she reminded him. 'Besides, I'll get paid for this! I'll meet people, watch them come and go all day — you can't know what that means to me.'

Well, he could, considering that Dosie often never saw another human being for months on end, and these were mostly trail-dusty desert wanderers with nothing to say that she was interested in. 'Hope it all works out,' Jake said, swinging aboard his horse once again.

Dosie frowned just a little. 'I hope everything works out for you, too, Jake.'

'I'll come back by and let you know what happened,' he said.

'Will you?' she asked, coming nearer, bedroll under her arm, hat tilted back as she lifted her eyes to his. The rising moon painted a soft golden aura around her head. 'And how long should I wait to see if you ever come back?' She paused, took in a deep breath and slapped the blue roan on the shoulder.

'Go on — get out of here.'

9

Jake thought he knew the trail to Belmont from there, but to be sure, he asked a couple of men on the street of the village, and they pointed out the road for him. The men acted as if that was a pleasant interruption in their routine. Alma was that sort of town. Jake wondered how anyone could live there.

He walked the blue roan out of town, guiding it south and west. He rode by moonlight along a wagon-wide road which wove through another stand of cottonwood trees and then straightened out as it met flat desert stippled with agave, yucca, clumps of nopal cactus and creosote bush. He was alone on the desert in the silent night, the moon gliding high. It could have been a pleasant ride, he reflected, were it not that he was headed back toward a troubled world.

Samuel Blaine certainly hadn't forgotten about being robbed, nor had the mine owners who had trusted him with their money, nor the miners themselves who had trusted their bosses to come up with their pay when it was due. None of these would be shy about bracing Jake Worthy with a gun or offering him the opportunity to stretch his neck on a length of hemp.

Still it had to be done. He had to get that constant little demon off his back. Even had he wished to keep the stolen money, what good would it do him in this country? A drifting man, an ex-convict, waving around that kind of cash would soon draw suspicion. It was return the money or spend the rest of his days riding hard and hiding well — a lifestyle that did not appeal to him. The problem was how to return the money without getting himself deeper into this mess.

Morning was soon enough to try to sort that out again. For now he rode on, the blue roan moving lazily beneath him, the desert pale beneath the moon. After some time he caught himself yawning and began to look for a place to camp for the night. There were few sheltered, hidden spots available to him on this treeless, featureless land, and he did not wish to veer far from the road; he didn't know the country well enough to travel on instinct. The moon was already beginning to fade behind the mountains and if Jake didn't need rest, the horse obviously did. Its gait had become a weary shamble by now.

It was certain that he was not going to reach Belmont on this night. Jake saw a crooked dark scar across the land and recognized it for what it was, a storm-cut arroyo, probably dry for eleven months of the year. It was deep enough to conceal his horse and as safe a place to hide as he was likely to run across on the far desert plains. Guiding the roan that way, he eased the horse down into the declivity. He rode a little way north, taking himself well off the main road. The arroyo forked off and he flipped a mental coin, following the gorge to his right. Ahead he saw a clump of live oak trees, black against the blackness of night. These would supply a little more in the way of concealment, and this was where he planned to spend the cold night.

Jake swung down stiffly, loosened the cinches of his saddle, but did not remove it from the roan's back. There was no telling how quickly he might have to leave. Again, he slipped the bit from the roan's mouth but left the bridle in place, tying the ends of the reins to a low branch of a dusty oak. Kicking aside some of the small, sharp live-oak leaves and dry fallen twigs, he spread his blankets on the ground and lay back to peer up at the starry sky through the branches of the tree.

'Welcome to my house,' a voice said, from out of the shadow-pooled night and Jake stiffened, letting his hand drop toward his holstered Colt. The voice chuckled a little. 'There's nothing to fear, friend. I'm the peaceable sort.'

'I can't see your face,' Jake said uneasily.

'It's not much to see,' the stranger said. 'I can't see yours either, but I recognize the horse you're riding — and your voice.'

'How could you — '

'Easy, I spent months talking to you in the dark while we were locked in together, and I know Bill Davenport's horse when I see it.'

'Grove! Eric Grove?' Jake asked with sudden recognition.

'It's me,' his former cell mate replied, shifting just enough in his bed to pinpoint his position among the deep shadows cast by the trees.

'Well, if this isn't something,' Jake said, still unsettled, but somehow relieved. 'Can you tell me — ?'

'I guess I could tell you quite a bit, Jake,' Grove answered. 'But if you don't mind, I'd rather let it rest until morning.'

That suited Jake Worthy. He was

tired, stiff and needed rest badly. He let his gun hand relax and fall away from his pistol, then tugged his blanket up under his chin and let the stars blink away, his eyes closing heavily.

Morning was a wash of pinkish-orange light which glowed in the eastern sky and was defeated by the cool shadows of the gulch where Jake lifted his head warily and searched the oak brush for Eric Grove. He could not have dreamed that the man was there with him. An alligator lizard scuttled across Jake's bed and paused to eye him with its snake eyes. Jake brushed it aside and rose to stretch out the night-stiffness. The blue roan, still tethered nearby, eyed him hopefully, silently pleading for grass and water.

Jake rose, slipped the roan its bit, cinched his saddle and untied the horse from the tree. There was a faint smell of smoke drifting on the slight morning breeze and after a minute, Jake came upon Eric Grove, crouched over a morning camp-fire.

'Coffee's boiled,' Grove said amiably. 'Like a cup?'

'Of course,' Jake answered. 'Have you seen any place the horses can graze and find a swallow of water?'

'Sure. That's one of the reasons I settled in here. Drink your coffee, and I'll show you where I keep my horse.'

The pond was little more than a scum-covered depression no more than eight feet wide, but the blue roan seemed unconcerned, nuzzling the green material away and drinking from it. 'There's grass a little way along,' Eric Grove told Jake. 'Let your horse eat what it wants of it — I won't be coming back this way again.' He laughed and then sat on the broken down sandy soil along the wash, in the morning shade.

'Have a rough time of it, Eric?' Jake asked, joining the older man, as the horse continued to drink.

'It was a bit of hell, Jake,' Eric said, tossing a small stone in the direction of a mesquite bush. 'Back in Belmont our horses had been cut loose, as you know.

Bill let us scatter to find whatever mounts we could. Then we were to join him in that alley across from the freight office. Sparky Finnet made a poor choice — the horse's owner was standing not fifty feet away from where it was tied. The man cut loose with his pistol. The bullet didn't hit Sparky, but it sure roused the townspeople. At about the same time a kid came out of the freight office and started yelling that it had been robbed.

'We slapped spurs to our horses and hightailed it. They came chasing us. More men than you would have thought lived in Belmont. So, all that day and the next we were riding as hard as we could trying to catch up with you and Yvonne at the same time as the stirred up townspeople were chasing us.

'It seemed like it would never end. Finally,' Grove told him, as he wiped out the sweat brim of his hat with a dirty kerchief, 'Bill Davenport caught lead from a man with a rifle and a good eye. It punched through him high on the shoulder. Bill couldn't ride no more. I suppose they arrested him, I don't know. Me and Sparky decided to split up and ride on, not chasing you any longer, but just trying to escape with our lives.

'Davenport, he was mad as hell, but he could see that the game was up. We left him sitting on a low knoll with twin oak trees growing on it, a rifle in his hands. Me, I ended up in Alma. I don't know where Sparky got off to. He said he knew a man who would put him up for a while. But only him. He didn't want the both of us riding out there.'

'I can see that,' Jake said. Rising to his feet, he went to catch up his horse and lead it to grass. Eric Grove followed along, practically in his footprints.

'Where's Yvonne?' Grove asked a little sharply.

'She caught a train East,' Jake answered. 'For all I know she's in Kansas City or St Louis by now.'

The horse munched dry grass. Jake withdrew to the shade of the dusty trees and leaned against the trunk of a shaggy old oak.

'She just went, no complaints?' Eric Grove asked doubtfully. Jake could follow his eyes, and by now he was certain that Grove had spotted the green satchel tied to his saddle. Grove pursed his lips thoughtfully, perhaps wondering if Jake had murdered the woman for the money. It was certain that he was giving the loot some thought, because, as Jake began to ready the blue roan for the trail, Grove commented, 'That's a lot of money. It was a lot when there was four of us. A two-way split would make a big payday.'

Jake faced Grove, looking across his horse's back, the rising sun glaring into his eyes.

'I'm taking it back,' Jake said. There was resolve in his words, but Grove just laughed.

'I know you're joking, but, Jake, don't try to cut your old partner out of a share. You and me were always friends.'

'No, we were two men who happened

to be stupid enough to get arrested at the same time.' Jake shook his head. 'I'm going back to Belmont and taking the money with me.' He swung into leather. 'Don't get any ideas about trying to stop me, Eric. Do you want me to tell you what happened to Sparky Finnet? That place that he was going to use as a hide-out — it was there and he tried to take the money from me. Now he's buried in a dog's grave.'

'You took Sparky Finnet, one on one? I don't believe it, Jake. Sparky had seen you shoot — remember? He was in that saloon the day you got the gambler. I just went along with the talk that you were some sort of slick gun hand so as to keep you alive. Remember what kind of shape you were in when we found you back in the White Mountains? If I hadn't talked you up to Bill Davenport, you'd be up there now, your bones bleaching.

'That's what I meant when I said I've been a friend to you. Now' — he approached Jake's horse with a fixed smile on his face as Jake swung aboard — 'let's talk seriously about the money.'

'That's as serious as I want to get,' Jake said, and he turned the horse's head away. Grove's hand shot out catching the roan's bridle.

The horse reacted angrily, twisting away and bucking, unseating Jake from the saddle. He slipped to the earth on the side away from Grove. The roan remained in place only because Grove had a fierce grip on its bridle still, yet it was angry and eager to be away from whatever sort of game it was that the men were playing.

'Get up, Jake,' Grove shouted. 'I'm going to have to kill you if you don't let me take that money now.'

Still Grove did not have himself set properly to shoot. He refused to let go of the horse's bridle and he was jerked this way and that. Jake was not set either. He rested on hands and knees behind the horse. He could see Grove's hectically moving legs under the horse's belly. Jake had his own gun in his hand, reluctant to use it, but Grove had as much as said it was one of them or the other. He would prefer not to be the one who died.

He felt compelled to give Grove a warning. 'I'm going to shoot, Eric!'

'Go ahead, gunfighter!' Grove was still puffing hard as he tried to restrain the roan. With the intention of wounding, but not killing Grove, Jake took aim at one of the man's dancing legs and fired off from beneath the horse's belly. Grove howled in pain and a blood spot appeared on his twill pants just below the right knee. The horse had not been hit by the passing bullet, but some of the blow-by from the fired weapon must have scorched its underbelly. It reared up in distress, shaking Grove's hand away and ran off into the clotted brush of the ravine bottom.

Jake got to his feet to face Grove who was grimacing with pain, his hand still holding his pistol firmly. Grove had lost his hat and his hair hung across his eyes, eyes that were filled with pain and ugly rage.

'Why'd you shoot me?' he demanded.

'If you don't know, nobody does,' Jake answered firmly.

Grove's chin was quivering with outrage. 'I don't have the time to fool with you, Jake. I got to catch up that horse, and I don't figure you're going to stop me.' Then without another word he leveled his Colt at Jake and fired.

Jake had already begun to move aside and, as he twisted and sprang to his right, Grove's bullet spun through the fabric of his shirt beneath the left armpit, missing the target by inches. Without conscious thought, Jake fired back even as he tripped and began to fall to the sandy earth. He saw Grove fling out his hands, saw his mouth open wide, saw him hit the ground at the same time as Jake did.

Sitting up against the sandy soil, Jake cocked his weapon again. Grove was on his knees facing him. His weapon was nowhere to be seen. An annoyed mockingbird swooped low over them as if it were trying to end the ruckus. Jake rose and walked to where Grove rested against the ground, his angry eyes hot enough to sear. Jake's shot had not been a killing one, but he could tell from the pinkish froth now leaking from Grove's lips that the bullet had tagged lung tissue.

Men had been known to drown internally with that sort of wound. 'Looks like you got me,' Grove said around the blood. 'We both know I won't make it. Have mercy and finish me off.'

'We'll try and get you to a doctor,' Jake replied, and Grove laughed loudly, his laugh interrupted by a choking, racking cough.

'Sure,' Eric Grove said bitterly. 'You start looking around in the trees for one and I'll try to figure out what to tell him when he gets here.'

Grove couldn't support himself any longer. His head bowed and he toppled over on to his side. Jake took him under the arms and towed him into the shade of the trees as the sun rose higher and heated the air in the narrow gully. Jake folded Grove's blanket, forming a pillow out of it and then sat down himself not far from the wounded outlaw. Grove trembled, his limbs twitched. His eyes carried a different expression now — a sort of pleading look.

He wanted Jake to finish him off before the pain got any worse as the shock wore off. The thing was, Jake couldn't do it. He may have become a killer, gunslinger, outlaw, but he could not bring himself to take a man's life like that. Feeling useless, beaten, guilt-ridden, Jake sat his gallows watch for another hour until he could no longer hear Grove's murmurs, the strangling of his lungs, and his body had gone motionless.

There was a trail of dead men stretched out behind him. The two young sheep men in Robles, Sparky Finnet and now Eric Grove. Jake shook his head, disgusted with himself although he knew that he could not have avoided any of the incidents. All he could dwell on was the fact that he was now a multiple murderer, a robber and a kidnapper. He would be lucky if he could find a place to roost where he could sleep through the night without imagining approaching footsteps. And there seemed no way out of the tangle. Still he would try to find a way.

First the stolen money — that had to be returned. So, feeling nothing like a famous gun hand, he walked along the sandy bottom of the brush-clogged gully until he found his horse standing in confusion in a clump of greasewood. The horse was wary but it patiently allowed Jake to readjust its bridle and check the cinch straps again.

Overhead Jake caught the dark circling silhouette of a buzzard in the pale-btue sky. Soon other devil birds, many of them, would come. Jake was briefly regretful that he had left Eric Grove to lie where he had fallen, but he knew that Grove would not have bothered to scratch out a grave for him.

Jake took the time to strip Grove's horse of its gear and set it free, then he settled himself into the saddle, tugged down his hat against the glare of the sun, and continued along his way across the sterile desert toward the town of Belmont feeling not like a dangerous man, but like a fool or a toy of the gods.

* * *

It was early evening when he trailed into the town of Belmont where it all had started and where it must somehow end. He reined up at the edge of town and, under a dusky sky already under the silver assault of stars, reviewed his options. Try to confide in a local lawman? No, there were too many potential charges against him. Try using a go-between as Dosie had suggested? Who? Who was there to trust with the money? Sending a note would only result in a trap being set for him.

Jake didn't like it, but it seemed that

180

the best, or only option was to find the freight-line owner, Samuel Blaine, at home and simply hand over the money. No discussion, no long conversation, just hand him the satchel and leave town quickly before anyone else could arrive to interfere.

It would work, or had the best chance of anything he could think of, simply because it was simple. Blaine, probably settling down to dinner, would answer the door, not wearing a gun in his own home. Jake would not introduce himself or explain anything. Just hand over the stolen money and be gone as a befuddled Blaine paused to open the bag and see what it was. Jake would already be on his way out of town, too rapidly for anyone to gather a posse.

He rode ahead along a mostly empty street. He passed a trio of cowboys riding from one saloon to the next. They paid him no mind. They were too busy with their own loud conversation that had something to do with a girl named Cheryl Ann.

Most of the store fronts were dark. There was a lantern burning in a boot-maker's shop. There were two men standing on the corner, sharing a bottle of whiskey. They had the appearance of miners, twill caps, heavy laced boots, overalls. Jake drew the horse in and sidled toward them.

'Do you boys know where Samuel Blaine lives?' he asked.

'Why, does he owe you money, too?' one of them shot back. Jake answered with a smile. 'No, I've never met the man.'

'You're lucky.' was the answer. His friend was the more sober sort. He lifted a pointing finger. 'The next street up, you'll see a road headed off south — the left as you're riding — take it about a half-mile. It's a white two-story house.'

Jake nodded his thanks and started the horse on again. Behind him the strangers had already forgotten about him. At least Blaine lived well out of town, isolated from it. There would be fewer interested eyes to note his arrival. As the lights of Belmont faded behind him into the night, Jake found himself fighting back an uncertain anxiety. To simply hand Blaine his money was the same as accusing himself of robbery and kidnapping. Be that as it may, he meant to be done with his chore on this night. He was sick and tired of worrying about the green satchel and its contents.

He had already determined that by the time Blaine could take the satchel and open it to examine what it held, Jake would be back on his horse, vanishing into the night. There was no reason that this should not work. But then, so many things had not been working out well for him lately.

He saw the large white house standing alone on a knoll. There were five or six horses in a pen not far away, in a small oak grove. These lifted their heads in curiosity, raising the blue roan's interest, but it did not whicker a warning that could have been heard in the house. It was somewhat weary again, its head slightly lowered as they approached the pole hitch rail in front of the house.

There was a light on within, and someone peered out from the corner of a curtain on hearing the horse's arrival, so the house was occupied. Jake swung down, secured the horse only loosely to the rail and untied the green satchel from the pommel where it seemed to have been tied for years.

Jake stood motionlessly in front of the house, wondering if he had made a huge mistake, but this was the plan he had settled on and, after glancing around to assure himself there was no one about in the yard, he walked up the front steps the white door of the Blaine house, reminding himself of his plan.

'Mister Blaine?' he would ask, and if the man nodded or answered in the affirmative, Jake would press the satchel on him and say only, 'For you'. Then turn and quickly depart. There would be no time for Blaine to react.

Feeling only moderately comfortable with the plan, Jake steeled himself, knocked on the door and waited. Footsteps approached, leather heels clicking against wood flooring. It swung open on well-oiled hinges and Jake found himself standing face-to-face with Yvonne Blaine.

10

'Come on in,' Yvonne said. 'In fact, you'd better — there's a gun trained on you.'

Glancing to his left toward the head of a short corridor Jake saw Bill Davenport, one arm in a sling standing with a pistol leveled at him. Davenport gestured with his pistol. 'You heard the lady. Get in here!'

Yvonne, dressed in a long white dress with black embellishments on the sleeves, backed away from the door far enough for Jake to enter. He started to ask, 'How did you get . . . ?'

'Those trains run both ways, you know,' Yvonne answered.

'You've saved us a lot of trouble, Jake,' Davenport said, coming forward. 'We've been wondering how we were going to track you down. Where are the boys? Have you seen any of them?'

'Who?'

'Grove and Sparky Finnet,' Davenport said impatiently, stepping nearer. 'You remember them, don't you? They went off to try to catch you after I was shot.'

Jake shrugged, 'I had to shoot them,' he answered. He saw Davenport and Yvonne exchange a glance. He told Yvonne, 'I thought your father would be here.'

'He's at work. Am I glad you showed up, Jake. You can't imagine how hard it would have been on me to be a penniless girl from the West. I couldn't have endured it.'

'What's the split?' Davenport asked, more directly. 'Or have you already taken out your cut?'

'No, I haven't,' Jake replied. 'You can lower that pistol, Bill. I don't want any of the money — I never did. I decided to try to give it back to Yvonne's father. I can see now that's not going to happen. So take it! I just don't care anymore,' he said, moving near enough to Yvonne to force the satchel on her. 'I guess I can live with my conscience if you can live with yours. Take the money and be damned, the two of you!

'Step aside, Bill,' Jake said in a different, lower tone of voice. 'I've done what I came here to do. Now I'm walking out of here.'

Yvonne had snapped the valise open and was now holding up a sheaf of bank notes to show Bill Davenport. 'A gift from heaven, Bill. Now we don't have to go hunting for him. He just walks right in and turns it over.'

'And now I'm walking out, as I said,' Jake grumbled. 'From now on the money is your problem.'

Bill Davenport said, 'I believe he means it.'

'Sure he does,' Yvonne said with a harsh little laugh. 'How could he turn us in without implicating himself? Besides, he has a little girl in a frilly pink dress waiting for him at home, remember?'

'I'm leaving,' Jake said. 'Don't try it

with me, Bill.' He nodded at Davenport's pistol.

Perhaps Bill had a mind to, but it would have been more trouble to explain to the law than it was worth. Maybe it was Jake's casual mention of shooting both Finnet and Eric Grove that shifted his mood, maybe the realization that there was nothing to be gained. They had the money: why take the risk?

Bill went so far as to holster his gun and walk toward Jake. He made a gesture that might have been an offer to shake hands, but did not go through with it. Smiling, Davenport asked, 'Is that my blue roan you're riding, Jake? I thought I saw it coming up to the house.'

'That's it.'

'Well, you just keep it, Jake. My arm won't be any good for riding for awhile . . . besides, we plan to spend our time riding the rails for now.'

Jake nodded, but his eyes were on Yvonne. He knew that smile, knew that

Davenport would not be the one holding that money in the end. Davenport had a thing for the sleek beauty, but Yvonne, especially now that she had what she needed to maintain appearances, would still be thinking about the cultivated, clever young men back East. There was no place in her life for Bill Davenport, but the outlaw just did not see that.

None of it was Jake's problem.

'Thanks for the horse,' Jake said, and retreated to the porch before Bill could change his mind. He walked rapidly across the damp grass to where the blue roan stood and swung aboard, riding as quickly as possible into the surrounding cloak of night. Just as he cleared the yard he heard a jeering call from Yvonne who had come out of the house, still clutching the green satchel with both arms.

'Kiss her for me, Jake!' she jeered.

Jake wondered if he would ever kiss Becky Holland again, but there was always hope. An hour along the trail he slowed the big blue roan to a walk and turned off on to the road leading to Rio Lobo.

By following the Rio Lobo itself the next morning, he was able to cut off a good five miles toward the town to which the river had lent its name. Rio Lobo, the river, was running shallow, and perhaps no more than twenty feet wide from bank to bank, but it sparkled prettily in the new sunlight and the willow trees flanking its shores gleamed at their tips, swaying in the fresh breeze. A few fish leapt from the water, flashing silver in the sun as Jake walked the blue roan across the river.

Then he was on to the east road as it was called, although following the meandering river it was at times on every point of the compass. The chaparral was high but thin, crowding the trail. Jake encountered a mule deer doe and her twin fawns going to water or coming from it. All three lifted their muzzles and blinked into the sunlight at him before taking fright and crashing off through the brush.

On a rise in the hills to the west now he could make out lazily rising smoke and see the shoulders of a few buildings. That was the town of Rio Lobo, but Jake continued his way along the well-remembered trail.

He found himself slowing the horse unconsciously, and when the Pasadena Fork was reached, he halted it entirely. What had happened to him? He had suddenly gotten cold feet. All of his planning, his dreaming of Becky Holland, his rush to get back to Rio Lobo, and now he was suddenly uneasy about seeing her again.

Maybe that was natural after so long a time. Each time he had returned before, she had welcomed him as if no time had passed, so perhaps he was concerned about nothing. The more time he spent thinking about it, the later it would make him. Setting his jaw, Jake urged the horse on down the south fork, the one leading to Becky Holland's little house in the hollow.

The two black oak trees still stood in front of the house, casting their blankets of shade. A yellow yard dog Jake did not recognize came out from under the little white cottage to yap at them and then slink away, tail tucked between its legs. The wind whispered through the oak trees and a pair of mockingbirds got into a noisy squabble somewhere among their branches.

The front door to the house swung open and Becky Holland came out on to the porch, wearing a pretty white dress. The sun gleamed on her golden hair. She held up her hand to shield her eyes and took a step back. Then, smiling shyly, she stepped down from the porch and crossed the yard, holding up skirt and petticoat.

One hand touched Jake's leg hesitantly as he sat his saddle. 'Tie your horse up. I've got coffee on the stove,' she said, her musical voice sounding only slightly surprised. Jake watched her turn around and scurry away. How a woman could look so pretty at this time of the morning amazed him. Had she been sitting up, knowing that he was bound to arrive? It was a puzzle.

Jake looped the reins around the sagging hitch rail and left the roan to nibble at what little grass it could reach. Scraping his boots off, Jake removed his hat and entered the familiar house. He crossed the braided rag rug and went into the small, white kitchen where Becky was bent over the iron stove, and took a seat at the round table.

'It took you a long time,' Becky said without turning to face him.

'I know, but, Becky, that was the last time. It couldn't be helped.'

'I waited at the stage station every day — eventually I gave it up. People shook their heads as if I were a fool.'

'I'm so sorry. Maybe when I tell you what happened — '

'I don't think I want to hear it,' Becky snapped. She walked to the table, taking short, choppy steps and placed a white mug on the table in front of Jake. 'You always have an explanation. I always accepted it because I know who you are. Even this last time when you were sent to prison, I believed you. I should have quit you then, but I couldn't do it by way of post. That wouldn't have been right. Anyway' — she tossed her head — 'I felt that I owed you one last chance when you got out. All you had to do was step on the stagecoach and come home. Couldn't you even do that for me, Jake?'

There were tears at the corners of her eyes now. He couldn't remember ever feeling this small. 'You see,' he began, trying to explain himself in some way she might understand. He had not tasted the coffee which had seemed so appealing minutes ago; he only turned the cup in his hands. Before he could go on, Becky interrupted him.

'Your horse has a bullet hole in its ear.'

'Yes, I know, you see — '

'At least I hope it is your horse,' Becky said. Her tone of voice was one he had never heard from her before, not even in the worst of times. Why was that? Had he disappointed her that much, made a bitter woman of her? Jake kept his eyes turned down to the table.

'It's my horse now. A man named Bill Davenport made a gift of it to me.'

'Bill Davenport, the outlaw!' Becky asked. Jake had forgotten that Davenport was already carrying quite a reputation in this part of the country before Jake had even met him. 'And where did he steal it?'

'Look here, Becky,' Jake said with more emphasis than he had intended, 'I can clear this all up for you if you'll just let me talk.'

Becky rose from her chair and swung her head slowly from side to side as if her neck pained her. 'I've heard enough tales from your lips to last me a lifetime, Jake. It's time to say enough is enough.' She hesitated and then added, 'Besides, I have other things to do today.'

'Please . . . ' Jake's vision blurred

suddenly. He was looking at her through a hazy light. Not really intending to, he grabbed her arms and stood her in front of him. His voice raised. 'If you'll just give me a few minutes — '

'Step away from that girl!' a shaky voice called from the open front door and, turning his head, Jake saw a man of about his height, a few years younger, dressed in a town suit, step across the threshold. The anger in his eyes was apparent.

'Oh, Austin,' Becky said, rushing toward him. 'I'm sorry — I thought I could handle him.'

'You are Jake Worthy, aren't you?' the young man demanded imperiously.

'I am,' Jake had to admit.

'My name is Austin Blaylock.' He had his arm across Becky's shoulders. She watched Jake anxiously, her body trembling. 'Miss Holland has consented to become my wife. I would suggest, Worthy, that you absent yourself from this property.' He added, 'I won't have

197

to get rough with you, will I?'

Jake looked at the earnest, narrow young man and shook his head.

'No, you won't. I know when I'm beaten.'

Jake walked across the floor and eased past them, catching a single glance from Becky Holland. It might have meant anything, but it no longer mattered. The man, whoever he was, would probably do a better job of providing for Becky than Jake ever could have. He stepped into leather and guided the blue roan out of Becky's yard.

No one stepped out on to the porch to watch him go.

* * *

The road back was torment. The day was bright, the breeze gentle, but Jake felt lost on a trail he knew well. He was a man who had ridden a rough road only to arrive at a place he had not intended to be. It — whatever he had been searching for — was gone: a mirage whisked away from before his eyes.

For a time Jake rode angrily, but he could not sustain his anger. Becky had made her choice, it seemed, and it probably had been the right one. He could not even recall the face of his competitor. What did it matter? He would never see him again. Nor Becky Holland. It was simple, taken all in all: he had had his chance and ruined it. There was no one but himself to blame. That's always a difficult conclusion to accept; it's so much easier when there's someone else to blame.

The road beside the Rio Lobo now began to rise out of the hollow where Becky's little cottage sat, and the day grew warmer. Puffs of dust rose from the horse's hoofs with each step. In his eagerness to reach Becky Holland's house Jake had failed to treat the horse as it deserved. It needed water and grass if it could be found.

Well, he thought, watching the sun

glint off the face of Rio Lobo, he was riding beside flowing clear water. He patted the blue roan's neck.

'I'll take care of you. Let's find us a little shade if we can, and some graze.'

Ahead now as the road dipped down again, Jake spotted a small park where a group of mature cottonwood trees stood, their leaves turning silver in the bright sunlight. Jake guided the horse that way, riding across a stretch of low-growing, but still green grass. Passing through the patchy shade of the mottled cottonwoods, he walked the horse to the edge of the river which murmured in its passing as the trees seemed to sigh in the breeze. The ancient language of the place was restful. The challenging voice he heard next was not.

'Hello, Jake Worthy! You are a hard man to find.'

Jake spun around, his hand dropping toward his holstered Colt, but he was already covered by the intruder's weapon. Jake looked once, twice, at the middle-sized man with reddish hair and at the gash across his skull where it had been parted, sprouting pure white hair.

'Quirk!' Jake said with surprise. The gambler from Tucson smiled faintly.

'So you do remember me?'

'Yes. I don't forget a man who cheats me at cards . . . or anything else. You're a long way from Tucson, Quirk.'

'A long way,' Ned Quirk said, carefully spacing out his words.

'Mind telling me what it is you want?' Jake asked. The blue roan was drinking peacefully from the river. A trio of teal ducks floated near the opposite bank, occasionally dipping their heads to dive. The leaves of the trees surrounding them fluttered in the breeze. It might have been peaceful, pretty here, but Jake was feeling too intense to note any of it. He knew what Quirk wanted. There was only one thing he could possibly want.

'To kill you,' Ned Quirk said, matter-of-factly.

'But . . . ' Jake began. Quirk was not

listening. He went on with his own speech.

'I got laughed out of town. There was no working there anymore. I had to wear bandages on my head even after the doctor got through stitching my scalp up. The story followed me everywhere and even when I finally got the bandages removed, I had this souvenir,' Quirk said, fingering the furrow running across his head.

'It could have been avoided if you hadn't bottom-dealt me those last two cards,' Jake pointed out. 'And you did draw first.' But the man was not in the mood to consider logic. Quirk's eyes grew thoughtful, but he was not thinking about what Jake had said.

'I knew when you were to be released from prison, and I made my way down there. An agreeable guard told me that you were going to catch the morning stage to Rio Lobo. Said he'd heard you had a girl back here. So I watched for you at the stage depot, waiting for my chance.' The gambler looked briefly enraged.

'You never showed up. By asking around I found out that you had used your release money to buy a horse and had ridden off to the east. I got a horse of my own and started following you. It wasn't easy, but I tracked you into the White Mountains until I was near enough to lay a trap for you.'

'You ambushed me and killed my horse,' Jake said flatly. The little gambler's eyes were jumpy. The hand holding his gun moved jerkily. He was primed to kill, but he seemed to want to finish his story first.

'Sure, I did,' he said, and now a little speck of foam had appeared on his lower lip. He licked it away and shrugged unapologetically. 'I could have finished you off then and there — it was what I intended to do, of course. Unfortunately for me, those three friends of yours showed up and I was forced to take to my heels. Following you after that was impossible. I decided to wait for you here. I knew that you would come to Rio Lobo sooner or later to see that little woman of yours, I saw her at the depot waiting for you and I asked who she was and where she lived. I knew you'd be coming this way sooner or later.'

'Clever, aren't you?' Jake asked. That sparked Quirk.

'Clever enough so that I got here first and I'm the one holding a gun on you.'

Jake could see that there was no other way out and so he growled as he went for his Colt, 'So shoot me, damn you!'

Even knowing that it was coming, the gambler was slow to fire. He missed his mark, but not by much. Jake felt searing pain low on his side, felt the bullet crease the top of his left hipbone. He was jarred by the shot, turned slightly to one side by it, but his own bullet found its mark. The .44 slug tagged Quirk exactly where it had six months ago, but this shot was two inches lower. No one would ever notice the groove this bullet had caused in its passing. Entering Quirk's forehead, it had exited nastily from the rear of his skull.

Jake walked that way, panting, his hand clamped over the wound in his side. He knew that Ned Quirk was dead, had to be, but he approached the gambler with his pistol still cocked and ready. Approaching the still figure, Jake felt his knees go slack and then buckle and he went to his knees, hatless, to stare out at the unappreciated beauty of the day. How long he remained there on his knees, resembling a penitent sinner, he could not have said. But the life was trickling slowly out of him, and his side was on fire.

'Damn you,' Jake said in a low gravelly voice to Quirk who lay dead on the sandy earth, already gathering flies. Damn all of them! Quirk, Eric Grove, Sparky Finnet, Bill Davenport, Yvonne — Jake had wanted none of this. His plan was to be released from prison and return to a peaceful life with Becky Holland, not to become a killer of men.

He had had it. No, Jake was not going to die of his wounds, but the heart had gone out of him. Why bother to plan a life? Why bother to reform, to try to live an upright existence? They would not let you go. The little dark things were persistent and malevolent. They kept after you, only wanting to drag you down to their little bit of hell.

The nudging of his shoulder caused Jake to break from his unhappy reverie and return to his here and now. The blue roan stood beside Jake, muzzling his shoulder, reminding him of things to be done. With a groan and a short stumble, Jake walked in a slow circle until he found where Quirk had hidden his little pinto pony in the trees. Unsaddling the animal, he freed it to wander on its way.

Jake considered that he was like some Johnny Appleseed of horse flesh, wandering the West, freeing the ponies after he had gunned down their owners. Eric Grove's horse, the dun that Sparky Finnet had been riding, Yvonne's sorrel, and now Quirk's little pinto. He hoped that whoever found each of them considered it a lucky stroke of fortune and treated it well. He smiled at the thought, but there was no depth to his expression. There was nothing very much funny going on.

Pausing to look around after the pinto had trotted free, Jake saw the saddle-bags Quirk had been carrying and decided to have a look inside them. A towel, a suit of long johns, a razor and soap. And a stack of currency and a leather sack heavy with gold and silver coins.

11

Automatically glancing around, Jake squatted beside the cache of money although it caused the pain in his hip to intensify. The horse, tired of Jake's slow progress had returned to nibble at the sparse grass in the cottonwood grove. Jake's hands were trembling just a little as he counted the paper notes and then the hard money in the leather poke. All in all it added up to something like $2,200.

Jake whistled and then rose to stand for a long minute watching the steady passing of the Rio Lobo.

Whose money was it? he considered, although he knew the answer.

It belonged to a hundred nameless men — hopeful cowhands, desperate miners, city businessmen, casual drinkers, faceless bar girls, wanderers, lawmen, butchers and tradesmen. Anyone who could be taken in by a deft bottom deal. Ned Quirk had been a gambler, a crooked gambler, all of his life. He had taken pennies, dollars, hundreds from all those who were uninformed enough to sit down at a table across from him. Jake knew this and he knew that there was no one to return the money to.

Spend weeks on a trail to return five dollars to an unlucky cowhand, ten dollars to a passing stranger . . . it was an impossible task. For the first time, Jake Worthy decided that he had the right to profit from his crime. After all, it was Quirk who had set it all in motion, all the killing, the running, the hiding.

Finally Jake stood, shouldering the saddle-bags. He said all he had to say to the figure of a dead man, 'Thanks, Mr Quirk,' and limped toward his waiting horse, considering the money small compensation for the loss of what he had imagined to be his future life's happiness.

He had begun to think about Becky

Holland again on the road to the town of Rio Lobo, before the pain in his side and reality pushed her out of his mind. Would Becky look more favorably upon a criminal who had $2,200 in his pockets than she had upon one without a cent? That was very unlikely. She had already affixed a label to Jake Worthy, and the name on it was not pretty.

The sun was still high, though the sun was tending westward when Jake rode into the little town of Rio Lobo where everyone seemed to be going about his daily affairs, even if those included only drinking at one of the two saloons he passed.

Asking around for a doctor, he learned that there was none, but the town had a barber who was considered a steady hand with a needle and always carried a good supply of opium for pain. Knowing he needed some sort of help, Jake rode the length of the short street until he found the barber's shop.

He waited slumped in a wooden chair until the barber had finished shearing an old mountain man, parting and oiling his hair until the man resembled an actual citizen. The mountain man was pleased. 'First trim I've had in almost five years — you done a good job, Bert.'

Bert, the barber, walked nearer to Jake, shaking the hair from the cloth he had covered the mountain man with. 'You look like you can use a little more than a trim,' he said.

'I guess I can,' Jake said. 'I had a little accident back along the river.'

The barber had spotted the bloodstain low on Jake's side and was already tugging Jake's shirt out to examine the damage. 'Doesn't look like much,' he muttered. 'Not if we get it cleaned out and you keep it that way.'

The barber escorted a shirtless Jake Worthy to a back room which held a sink and a trestle table where Jake was invited to lie.

'Just grit your teeth some,' the barber said. 'Think you can handle a little pain?'

211

'If you're asking — no, I don't want opium.'

'Then get a grip on that rolled towel or something. I'll try to make this quick and easy.'

And it was. Washing the wound with soap and water, then applying carbolic, the barber sewed the loose skin up deftly. Wrapping a bandage tightly around Jake's hips, he pronounced his customer fit enough to go on his way. 'Just don't do any unnecessary stretching, and you should be fine.'

Stepping outside, Jake studied the long sky. He felt like traveling on, but it was growing late, and it made more sense to have the blue roan fed and rested. He meant to treat himself the same way. After a supper of beef steak, boiled potatoes and corn on the cob, Jake took a downstairs unit in a four-room hotel where he intended to catch up on his sleep.

First, however, he sat on his bed and recounted the money he had recovered from Quirk.

Twenty-four hundred dollars and fifty cents. Not a lot of money, perhaps, but it was about what an average cowhand would take over six years to earn. What to do with it now was the question. In the restaurant as he was eating, he had heard conversations going on at other tables. One man had found a strong vein of silver ore but found himself cash-short when it came to purchasing an ore-crusher. Another wished to start his own freight line but badly needed another wagon and a team of horses.

The opportunities were out there, Jake was beginning to understand. If he could invest $2,000 in something that had real potential, that would leave him with $400 to live on for at least a year. He told himself that he would not rush into any venture, but he was willing to explore any possibility.

Thinking of these things, he felt his head begin to nod, and Jake lay back and stretched out on his bed.

★   ★   ★

It was only an hour after sunrise that Jake found himself on the outskirts of Alma. The well-rested, well-fed blue roan had eaten up the rough, dry miles from Rio Lobo. Jake walked the horse along the street and swung down in front of the dry goods store where the proprietor — a short, round man in bifocals — was just opening his store for the day. Jake asked for the shirts and picked out a dark-blue, shell-style one.

'I'd like to wear it,' Jake said. 'Is there a place I can change?'

'Where you're standing is fine by me, unless you want me to turn my back. There's no one else in the store.'

Jake nodded and removed his faded, torn, road shirt. Getting it off and easing into the new one aggravated his wound a little, but not enough to start it bleeding again. The storekeeper watched Jake's obvious struggle to change. But he said only, 'Would you like me to wrap up your old shirt to take along to a laundry?'

'No, you can burn it as far as I'm

concerned. Have you got much in the way of kerchiefs?'

'Right over here,' the salesman said eagerly. There were all sorts there, flowered, silk, striped. Jake held a few of them up in front of his new shirt, then reached for a bright yellow kerchief. It looked almost like a cavalry scarf, but Jake liked the way it set off the dark blue of his new shirt. 'I'll take this one.'

'All right. Anything else this morning?' the clerk asked, his eyes glowing eagerly behind his glasses.

'Not today, thank you.' Jake peeled off some money from the thin roll he was carrying — the big money rode stashed away in his saddle-bags — and left the store.

The sun was bright in his eyes, but the brilliance of the day was not overpowering. It was still morning cool in the shadows. He saw a kid of ten or so squatted beside a wooden box in front of a neighboring saloon, and out of curiosity he walked that way. The kid looked up with hopeful eyes as Jake reached him.

'Need a dog, mister?'

Jake crouched down to look inside the box. Two rough-coated pups of uncertain parentage waited there. One of them yawned at Jake's appearance, but the other pup placed his front paws over the edge of the box, its white-tipped tail wagging furiously.

'They're good-looking little guys, aren't they? Think they're going to be big?'

'Their ma's shoulder is at least knee-high on a man,' the kid said. 'She had five pups. These are all that's left. This other one I promised to hold for a man who went into the saloon. Lord knows when I'll see him again. The one wagging its tail I'll give you for a nickel.'

'You already sold the other ones?' Jake asked, smiling at the kid who seemed to love the pups.

'Two of 'em,' he said a little ruefully. 'My dad told me it was time to get rid of them, they being too old to nurse.' His voice lowered a little and he glanced around. 'I still got my favorite hidden out in our barn.' He smiled. 'I know my dad, though, he'll give in and let me keep it.'

'So that makes this the last one,' Jake said, scratching the rough-coated pup with the white tip on his tail. It had begun trying to leap up toward Jake, its pink tongue licking at him wildly.

'He's the last, but he's a good one,' the boy said eagerly.

Jake stood, the pup still trying to reach him from the confines of the box. 'I think so, too,' Jake said. He dug a nickel from his pocket and passed it to the boy. 'Will you watch him one minute while I go back into the dry goods store?'

'Sure!' the boy, obviously pleased with the way his morning was progressing, said. 'Do you want me to cut you a length of this to use for a leash?' He held up a ball of twine.

'I suppose so. I might need it for a time.'

Jake turned away and returned to the store. When he came back he was carrying a yellow bandanna, identical to his own, and he tied it around the writhing neck of the clumsy pup.

'That ought to do it,' he said, and he removed the shaggy pup from the box.

'Be good to him mister,' the kid said, rising. 'Are you taking him far?'

'I don't know yet. It could be a long, long way.'

Jake tried walking the puppy along the boardwalk back to where the blue roan stood at the hitch rail. The dog bounded, leapt, paused to pee, nipped at the cuffs of Jake's jeans and circled around him, winding the twine around his legs. The boy watched their progress with some concern. Jake waved reassuringly to the kid. None of it bothered him. It was all normal pup behavior.

Jake's own behavior might not be considered so normal, but a man has to take a chance now and then.

He knew the way. It had not been that long ago since he had passed through the cottonwood grove and come upon the four tiny white cottages. The pup had ridden across the horse's withers, quite calm now after an initial bit of panic. It strained to lick Jake's hands frequently.

Walking the horse slowly through the grove, Jake came within sight of the cabin. A slender woman was on the porch, sweeping. Jake swung down from the blue roan and lifted the puppy down. It sniffed around excitedly for a minute and then fell in behind Jake as he made his way toward the cottage. There was no need for the leash. When they were within five paces of the porch Dosie heard them, or sensed them, and turned around.

Her eyes narrowed as she fixed her gaze on the two, man and dog, both wearing yellow bandannas, and she seemed to smile. She placed her broom aside.

'Well, Jake, I didn't expect to see you again. At least not so soon.'

He removed his hat. 'I just had some things to take care of.'

'And are they taken care of?' Dosie wanted to know.

'They're taken care of,' Jake told her, 'all of them.'

'I see,' Dosie said. Her arms were folded beneath her breasts. She watched as the puppy continued to snuffle around the yard. She smiled more deeply now, and asked, 'What brings you back this way, Jake?'

'I was just wondering . . . now that you've had a little time to think about it, if you've decided whether you might ever like to keep a dog.' He waved a hand toward the pup, 'So I brought you one.'

Dosie nodded sagely, seated herself on the parch, and answered, 'I'm not sure, Jake. That's something a person needs to think about seriously. Why don't you sit down here next to me, and we can discuss it a little more.'

The sun rode higher, the pup had begun digging a hole in the yard. Jake and Dosie had finished their conversation. The dog had found a home.

THE END

We do hope that you have enjoyed reading this large print book.

Did you know that all of our titles are available for purchase?

We publish a wide range of high quality large print books including:
Romances, Mysteries, Classics
General Fiction
Non Fiction and Westerns

Special interest titles available in large print are:
The Little Oxford Dictionary
Music Book, Song Book
Hymn Book, Service Book

Also available from us courtesy of Oxford University Press:
Young Readers' Dictionary
(large print edition)
Young Readers' Thesaurus
(large print edition)

For further information or a free brochure, please contact us at:
Ulverscroft Large Print Books Ltd.,
The Green, Bradgate Road, Anstey,
Leicester, LE7 7FU, England.
Tel: (00 44) 0116 236 4325
Fax: (00 44) 0116 234 0205

THE MAN FROM CHEYENNE

Jack Edwardes

The last man to wear a sheriff's badge has finally been driven out of Jackson Creek — so Jake Pierce plans to take over the town, backed by a group of vicious gunfighters. When Clay Harding rides in from Cheyenne to bring back the rule of law, he is sucked into a whirlpool of killing and the lure of gold. Knowing that he might never get back to Cheyenne, he can console himself with one thought: he might be able to shoot his way out of trouble . . .

DEVINE

I. J. Parnham

Pinkerton detective Nimrod Dunn is hired by Lieutenant Governor Maddox Kingsley to infiltrate an outlaw gang. But when Nimrod's cover is blown, an innocent life is lost in the raging gun battle. The fearsome US Marshal Jake T. Devine then sets about bringing the outlaw Cornelius to justice — but his methods are as brutal as those whom he pursues. With Devine's blood-soaked trail making a mockery of the governor's promise to clean up the county, Maddox must call on Nimrod's services once more — to kill Marshal Devine . . .

HELL COME CALLING

Josh Lockwood

Big Jim Wolfe rides into the town of Greasewood for a rest, but instead finds himself defending a family of Mexican sheep-herders from a power-hungry cattle baron. Jack Whelan has the town under his control and is ready to launch an all-out bloodbath in order to gain the rest of the valley. But the one thing he hasn't counted on is the deep-seated sense of right and wrong that Jim Wolfe lives by. He isn't a man to go looking for trouble, but he certainly won't walk away from it . . .

WHISPERING SKULL

Dean Edwards

In search of work, cow-puncher Jeff Stewart is heading south. Making his way through the strange, untamed landscape that fringes the arid desert; he is riding up into the maze of canyons when there is distant gunfire and a massive explosion. With the sound of bullets ringing in his ears, the naïve cowboy has no idea that the savage Barton gang is en route to the notorious prison, Fort Addams, to free their leader — and that soon Stewart and the gang will be on a deadly collision course . . .